THE LURKER FILES

FACELESS

by
Scott Ciencin

Random House Cyber Fiction
Random House · New York

To my beloved wife Denise for keeping me going during all the long hours this project required, to my agent, Jonathan Matson, who deserves a place at the round table for all his efforts, to Ruth Koeppel, Jim Thomas, and Mary Man-Kong, my editors, to Laura (Amy) Ciencin-Guild, to the Ratskellar dwellers—you know who you are, and to the Lurker…one day the mask will fall!

A RANDOM HOUSE CYBER FICTION BOOK PUBLISHED BY RANDOM HOUSE, INC.

http://www.randomhouse.com

Library of Congress Catalog Card Number: 96-68024
ISBN: 0-679-88235-9

Printed in the United States of America   10 9 8 7 6 5 4 3 2 1

Intro

Gia Gibson sat alone in her cramped dorm room. The only light came from the computer screen before her. Gia's fingers cruised over her keyboard as she "spoke" with Wally Deitz in a private chat room. His dorm room was only one floor above hers. She could have just gone upstairs to speak with him. But Wally was painfully shy in the real world. It was difficult to talk to him in person. On-line, as Beaker, he was relaxed and funny. She responded to him as Ripley.

> **Beaker:** yo baby baby waz up?
> **Ripley:** not me, that's 4 sure
> **Beaker:** talk to me, funky chunky monky, why RU:-(
> **Ripley:** Rat attack. Couldn't get through Hole in the Wall AGAIN
> **Beaker:** They dont know what theyr mizzing FB FB FB bleah!

Gia grinned. The first time she'd seen "FB" in a chat room, she'd had no idea what it meant. Later, she learned it was cybershorthand for "furrowed brow—angry!" Wally's show of outrage on her behalf was comforting. She'd been trying to get into the Ratskellar for months. The put-downs she'd endured at the door of the exclusive chat room had been especially cruel tonight. Still, she hadn't meant to get Wally so upset.

Ripley: (((Big hug!)))
Beaker: :-} oh my goodnezz oh my good-nezz. I'm blushing!
Ripley: U on call tonight?
Beaker: nope—some other computer geek gets to fix the crashes. Im off the clok
Ripley: you are NOT a geek, you are a GURU!!!
Beaker: yes maam…is my homegirl Peggy wit U ???
Ripley: it's only 11 at night, beakdude… she'll wait until I'm cruzin some snoozin before she comes home from her parenz
Beaker: sheZ been gone all weekend?
Ripley: A-ffirmitive on that…surprise visit home…ded prez run
Beaker: ah… ;-) up cloze an' personal to squeeze out da cash
Ripley: U sed it, I diden
Beaker: yez you did!!!

Gia sat back, smiling. She knew that her room-mate really enjoyed her visits home. But it was almost the end of the semester. Funds were running low. Gia was even worse off than Peggy when it came to her bank account. Even so, lack of cash wasn't what bothered her tonight. She was dying to get inside the Ratskellar. Ever since she'd arrived at Wintervale Univer-sity, she'd been reading about the Rat in the "Nibbles and Crumbs" section of the campus newspaper. True, she was only a first-semester freshman. But the Hole in the Wall recognized and sometimes rewarded those who refused to give up. Gia had an idea about how to get in, but she was going to need Wally's help.

Ripley: yo, Beakmeister
Beaker: comin at ya—whut you need, hmmmmmmmmm?
Ripley: I was thinking…maybe we could try a Rat attack together…

Gia waited for a response. She was asking Wally to come out of Wally World. The only way they could attempt to get inside the Rat together was if they sat side by side at one PC. Only Wally wasn't responding.

Ripley: Beakboy, you there?
Beaker: TTYL

Gia watched her screen in shock as Wally cleared out of their private chat room. His screen name vanished from the small box that listed who was in the room. "TTYL" meant "talk to you later." It wasn't like Wally to sign off so abruptly. She could hardly believe it.

Sitting alone in the near darkness of her tiny room, Gia wished that Peggy would show up already. Earlier, she'd been glad that her roommate was taking her time getting back to campus. There was only one computer in their room, and tonight she'd wanted it all to her-

self. Sunday night Rat rejection was getting
to be a ritual.

Peggy thought the Rat was cool, but she wasn't
obsessed with getting in. Not like Gia. But
the truth was, just about everyone at Wintervale was dying to see the Rat for themselves.
The chosen few who'd managed to get inside
said it was worth all the trouble.

Gia looked at the clock. A little after
eleven. Should she go upstairs and knock on
Wally's door? Apologize for making him uncomfortable? Or would that make things even
worse?

Come on, Peggy, she thought. You always know
the right thing to do in these situations.
Come back and get me out of this, all right?

Gia stared at her screen. She moved her mouse
around to prevent the screen saver from kick-
ing in. Certain that Wally wasn't coming back
to the private chat room, Gia moved her cursor
to the exit icon. But before she could double-
click, her screen suddenly went crazy! The
chat room's walls began to crack. A black pat-
tern raced across her computer screen like a
nightmare. The graphics on her screen became
warped and turned ugly Day-Glo colors.

Frantically, Gia pounded at her computer. But
her keyboard was locked up and her mouse was
no help at all. Gia watched helplessly as she
was yanked out of the chat room and sent rac-

ing from one Web site to the next—totally out of control!

Images flashed by too quickly for her to identify any of them. Gia suddenly became afraid that some kind of mega-virus had been downloaded into her system. Was her computer crashing?

Finally, all the weirdness cleared from her screen to reveal a block of text. Gia read a few lines, then drew back. It was a brutal first-person account of a college student's murder. The victim's name was Peggy Parrish. Her roommate!

Gia kept on reading. She couldn't stop herself. She knew one thing for sure: Whoever had written this trash was seriously messed up. Everyone loved Peggy. Only a sicko would dream of hurting her. What really worried Gia, though, was that this "diary entry" was dated two days ago—the day Peggy had left for her parents' house. Gia suddenly felt an urge to call Peggy's parents. Just to make sure that Peggy had gotten there in one piece…

Then suddenly the words vanished and were replaced by a rush of frightening images. People screaming and hiding their faces with their hands. Photographs of the dead staring out at her with blank eyes. With a sinking feeling of dread, Gia realized that one of the photos was of Peggy. She had been murdered exactly as the diary entry had described! Gia stared at the photo in horror. The text on her screen hadn't been some freak's twisted fantasy. It was real.

The image vanished as quickly as it had appeared, and the screen went black. Suddenly, an intruder appeared in Gia's room, but he didn't break through her door or window. He didn't pop out from under her bed or burst from her closet. Instead, he took the form of a single line of text on her computer screen. Fear rippled through her as she read the awful message.

Dethboy: I see you, Gia…YOU'RE NEXT.

Gia couldn't look at Dethboy's threat one second longer. She hit the computer's power button, and with a crackling pop the screen went black. Gia's cramped dorm room was cast into darkness. After a moment, her eyes adjusted to the moonlight, and she made her way over to the window. Pushing the curtains aside, she looked out at the woods behind Crane Hall. Not a soul was in sight. Trembling, Gia turned to face Peggy's unmade bed. It had been untouched since Peggy left two days ago. Gia shuddered. If the photos she'd seen were real, Peggy would never sleep in that bed again. Gia didn't want to believe it, but her roommate might be gone forever.

Suddenly, there was a knock at the door. Gia cried out and stumbled back. Her foot caught in the base of her chair, dragging it down as she fell. It landed on Gia's legs, pinning her to the cold hardwood floor. Gia's heart thundered. All she could think about was Dethboy. For all she knew, he might live right upstairs. Upstairs…Wally's room was upstairs. No! Wally was her friend…wasn't he?

The knock came again. "Come on out, Gibson! I know you're in there!"

It was a female voice. One Gia recognized. Relief flooded through her. She wriggled out from under the chair and flicked on the lights. When she opened the door, Jenny Dvorak stood waiting in the hall. Jenny was thin, blond, and beautiful. A sophomore sorority queen in a short black designer dress. Jenny always looked so grown-up, so sophisticated. Gia suddenly felt self-conscious in her over-sized sweatshirt, torn jeans, and bright red socks. To top it off, her hair was a mess. Gia groaned inwardly. She'd had some rough deal-ings with Jenny when she first arrived at Win-tervale. Jenny'd had it in for her. And Gia had never found out why. Hopefully all that was behind them.

"Tough day at the office?" asked Jenny with a wink, eyeing the overturned chair.

Gia smiled despite herself. "Oh. Um…" She crossed her arms, trying to think of something to say. She desperately needed to talk about what she'd just seen in Dethboy's lair. But could she trust Jenny?

Before Gia could make up her mind, Jenny pulled a sheet of paper from her little black purse. "Campus e-mail's all messed up," she said. "I got this in my mailbox by mistake. I printed it out for you."

Gia took the piece of paper and unfolded it. The sender was "Lean Machine." Gia'd never seen that screen name before—it could be anyone. But Gia recognized the name at the bottom of the letter. It was from Peggy. And it had been sent only an hour ago! Gia was stunned. According to what she'd seen on her computer screen, Peggy had been dead for two days.

To: Gia Gibson
From: Lean Machine

Snootchie Bootchie! Hey, Poodle Head! You won't believe what happened on my way home. I met this guy. He's GORGEOUS. And he's smart. And he's funny. Remember what you said you'd do if Darren ever noticed you were alive? That you'd just run away with him? And I said you were crazy? Well, I've met my own Darren. His name's Troy. You are NOT going to believe it. He proposed. And we're running away together. Guess you weren't so crazy after all!

Do me a favor? Let my parents know so they don't worry. I'll check back in a week or so. After the honeymoon. And get my homework, too, okay? Maybe you can upload it to me. I'll try to stay in touch. Troy's got this awesome laptop. But finding a phone jack on the road can be a nightmare. So I don't know if I'll be checking my e-mail or not. Just so you know, right now we're in Kansas and heading south. Do the Snoopy dance of joy for me! Miss you! ;-)

—Peggy Poodles

Gia didn't know what to think. A few minutes ago she'd been staring at a photo of her murdered roommate. Now she was reading an e-mail sent only an hour ago. From Kansas! And it was definitely from Peggy. Only Peggy knew about the Snoopy dance. It was something Gia and her mom used to do when Gia was little.

Suddenly Gia noticed that Jenny was looking at her strangely. She'd given her that look plenty of times when Gia had first arrived on campus, and it wasn't friendly. Gia was about to say good night when Jenny swallowed and said in a small voice, "I sort of read it. Sorry."

Gia winced slightly. That meant Jenny knew about her crush on Darren. Still, Jenny didn't look as if she were going to do anything bad with that knowledge.

"It's okay," Gia said. She'd totally misread Jenny, and it wasn't the first time.

"Are you all right?" Jenny asked.

Gia nodded. "Just had a bad connection online," she said. "That's all."

"Okay. Well...see ya," Jenny said, heading off down the hall. Gia went back into her room and got her keys. As she locked her door, she thought about going to see Marissa Valero, her floor's R.A. Marissa could handle any crisis. Gia truly admired her. But instead, she headed toward the stairs to find Wally. If anyone could figure out what had happened with the computer, it would be him.

Gia took the stairs two at a time. At the landing, she rounded the corner and plowed straight into someone coming down the other way. A pair of hands grabbed her. She gasped, frightened. Gia looked up and was relieved to see her friend Lee. Most people wrote off Lee as a brick wall with no neck and no brains. A dumb jock. But there was more to him than that. A lot more.

"Yo, it's the G!" Lee said. His huge hands dropped to his sides. "How ya doin'?"

Gia's shoulders sank. "Not great. I was just gonna see if Wally was around."

"He's MIA," Lee said. "I was supposed to borrow some books from him, but no one's answering the door. I thought he or Peter would be around, but—zip!"

Gia felt a little light-headed. Lee took her by the shoulders and sat her down on the stairs. "What's going on?" he asked.

Gia told him everything. Her attempt to get into the Ratskellar. Being pulled into Deth-boy's lair. Reading the account of Peggy's murder. Seeing her photo. The threat Dethboy made. Then she let Lee read the printed e-mail Jenny had delivered.

"You think I'm crazy?" Gia asked.

"No way," Lee said. "You're the sanest person I know. If you say you saw this stuff, then you saw it. No two ways about it. The question is, what'd you see? I mean, someone could have taken a photo of Peg and played around with it in the computer lab. It's amazing the stuff they can do."

"Yeah, I hadn't thought of that," Gia admitted. She felt a little better. "But Dethboy called me by my real name! How'd he know who I was?"

"I guess if he saw 'Ripley' on screen, well… You've been using that screen name for a while now. A lot of people know that's you. Maybe we should call campus security. Or the police."

Gia thought about it, and shook her head. "I don't know."

Lee put his arm around Gia's shoulders. "I've got an idea. Let's go back to your room and send an e-mail to this 'Lean Machine' address. We'll tell Peggy to call as soon as she gets the e-mail. That way you'll know she's okay."

Gia gave Lee a smile. "Good idea," she said.

"And after we send the e-mail," Lee added, "let's get out of the dorm for a while. Darren's having a party. Colonel Mustard's playing. You want to go?"

Gia didn't even have to think about it. Her
heart was ready to explode at the thought of
seeing Darren. A chance to be near Mr. Perfec-
tion? "I guess that wouldn't suck," she said,
smiling.

Lee nodded. "Cool. Let's go!"

They headed down the hall toward Gia's room.
For a second, she thought she saw a shadow
near the exit door. But when she looked again,
it was gone. It must have been her imagina-
tion...

2

"Yo, Lee!" Gia called out as she changed into yet another outfit. It was her third so far. "Where is this party, anyway?"

"Darren's having it at our frat house," Lee said from outside her door. "And I *know* you've got a thing for him. So lock and load, G! He can't notice you if you're not there."

Gia grabbed one last outfit. This would be the one, she decided, no matter what. She was glad she wouldn't have to spend the evening alone in her room after her encounter with Dethboy. And a chance to be near Darren was not to be missed! Without even looking in the mirror, she opened the door and braced herself for Lee's reaction.

"Dude!" Lee said, gawking at her.

"If that's what you think, I did something wrong," said Gia, smiling. She wore a tight-fitting black turtleneck dress that she'd picked up at the mall. Like the one Sharon Stone had worn to the Oscars. Her hair was pulled back and piled high on her head.

"You look great," Lee said. Suddenly, he seemed worried. "Um...Y'know, Jenny's dress looks a lot like that."

Gia froze. Lee was right. She'd just seen Jenny, and she'd also been wearing a black dress. How could she have forgotten?

Well, it was too late to change again now. Besides, she wanted to look good for Darren. "It'll be okay," Gia said, slipping on her leather jacket and locking her door.

Lee raised his eyebrows. "Whatever you say."

They left Crane Hall together. It was freezing outside. Gargoyles stared down at them as they crossed the campus. A block away from Darren and Lee's frat house, they started hearing music. By the time they got there, it sounded like an outdoor concert.

A half dozen guys sat around on the porch. When Gia and Lee approached, one of them sprang to his feet and held his hand out to stop them. Lee climbed the stairs anyway. The frat boy had a buzz cut and a goofy grin. His T-shirt read, I BRAKE FOR PHILOSOPHY MAJORS!

"Hold, brother!" Buzz said. "Do you know the secret word?"

Lee picked the freshman up and shook him a few times. "Get—*out*—of—*my*—*way*!"

"That works for me!" Buzz squeaked, making a feeble peace sign. Lee set him down and buffed the top of his head. "I've been touched by greatness!" Buzz exclaimed as he returned to his friends.

Lee looked over his shoulder and grinned at Gia. She smiled back, shaking her head.

Chaos reigned inside the frat house. Colonel Mustard was cranking in the cramped living room. Suddenly the drummer stood up in the middle of the song. He raised his sticks, threw his head back, and started to shake.

"He's channeling!" screamed someone in the crowd. The band stopped playing, and everyone became quiet.

The drummer moved one of his sticks back and forth slowly, eyes closed, as if he were in a trance. Gia looked at Lee and asked, "What are they doing?"

"Just watch," Lee said.

The drummer opened his eyes and pointed at a young man in the crowd wearing a black T-shirt and a fuzzy pair of bright red earmuffs.

"You have been chosen!" cried the drummer. Earmuffs threw his head back and howled. Then he made his way through the crowd and knelt before the drummer, who "knighted" him with his drumsticks. "You are now the Life of the Party! Do you have any words to inspire us?"

Earmuffs raised his hands in the air and shouted, "PARTY!!!"

"So let it be written, so let it be done!" cried the drummer.

The crowd exploded as the band started playing again.

"I'll take your coat!" Lee shouted over the din.

Laughing, Gia slipped out of her jacket. A number of guys immediately checked her out, and one of them actually gave her a thumbs-up. Jenny drifted by and saw Gia's dress. Her eyes narrowed, and she stormed off.

"You're bold," someone said in Gia's ear. "You're extra-bold!"

Gia spun around and saw Darren McKiernan standing before her, grinning. He was outrageously gorgeous, with a thick mane of dark hair and piercing eyes. He wore a grayish blue wool sweater, jeans, and black boots.

Gia was speechless.

"Don't worry about Jenny," Darren said. "She'll get over it."

"I knew she was wearing a black dress," Gia

shouted over the band. "I didn't think it would be a big deal!"

"It's not. Had any punch? Gotten anything to eat?" Darren led Gia over to the refreshment table. A frat boy ladled out some punch as Gia got some snacks.

"I've seen you around a lot," Darren said.

Gia was shocked. "You have?"

"Sure. You're working on the lit magazine. I do the covers."

"Oh, right!" Gia swallowed hard. "I tried to get on the student paper, but it's tough."

Darren nodded. "I know someone who could help. You want to talk to him?"

Gia looked around for Lee. He'd vanished with the coats. "Sure."

Darren led her to a room near the back of the frat house. He unlocked the door and stepped into the darkness. He flicked on the light, revealing a mini—computer lab.

"Shut the door, okay?" Darren said. "Don't want anyone wandering in."

Darren sat down before one of the computers and turned it on. As the machine booted up, he patted the chair next to him.

Gia couldn't believe she was alone with Darren. Leaving the door open slightly, she went over to sit beside him.

Darren's fingers flew over the keyboard. His keyboard was different than most Gia had seen. It had a separate group of keys labeled PF keys off to the far left hand side of the keyboard. These were program keys.

He entered the chat rooms, then made a run at the Rat. But instead of waiting for the Gatekeeper to quiz him, Darren hit a program key that activated some kind of macro. It took him past the Gatekeeper screen and into a chat room Gia had never seen before.

Gia noticed Darren's screen name listed in a small box with the other occupants of the chat room. Fratguy. It sounded oddly generic, like something any memeber from the frat could use.

"Wait a minute," she said. "This is the Ratskellar!"

Darren smiled and kept on typing. On screen, two people were talking in a language Gia didn't know. One word came up over and over again. "Meinichi." She wondered what it meant.

"I think that's Japanese," Darren said with a shrug. "I can't speak it, can you?"

Gia shook her head.

Darren poised his hands over the keyboard.
"There's a ton of little rooms off the Rat.
Wanna see some of them?"

"Definitely," said Gia. She glanced at Darren's fingers as he typed. He punctuated each
code with one of the program keys. As they
entered a new room, Gia began to wonder if it
was the program keys doing all the work.

> **Lord Myron:** as some weary bird without a
> mate, my weary heart is desolate
> **Flintztones:** <BURRRRRP!!!>
> **Pundit:** tis better to have loved and
> lurked than never to have lurked at all
> **Philstone:** anybodey got a mint?

"It's Lord Myron," Darren said. "He's obsessed
with the poet Lord Byron."

Darren switched them to another room.

> **Flatline:** spam, where you am, I'm a call-
> in' you out
> **Cappacola:** control, dude
> **Pundit:** actions speak louder than lurks
> **Spam I Am:** spam, ready to jam, what up
> :::)

"This Pundit guy's everywhere," Gia said.

"Yeah, we think there's a whole army of them,"
Darren replied. "Hold on, here we go…"

Darren took them into yet another room off the

Rat. "Now there's the fella we need."

> **Studpuppet:** The net obscures our identi-
> ties from all. So be who you want to be
> and explore and learn. A wise man named
> Ransom told me this.

"Oh, really?" Darren said as he keyed in a new
code to change his screen name. Gia was
stunned as Darren's screen name came up.
Raspuddin?! She'd heard that name before. He
was a total legend in the Rat.

> **Raspuddin:** When you're done, snatch the
> pebble from my hand, young grasshopper.
> **TK 2bad4u:** Hey, what the ho ha? What am I
> doing here?
> **Studpuppet:** Is this a challenge, oh less
> than serene and more than smelly one?
> **Raspuddin:** Yeah, and if I win...
> **Pundit:** Must be the lurk of the draw...
> **Raspuddin:** you owe me one

"You're Raspuddin?" Gia asked. "The Mad Monk
of the Rat?"

"At your service." Darren bowed slightly in
his chair. "I can't tell you who Studpuppet
is, but I know he's got some pull with the
newspaper. If I win, I'll get you on the
paper."

"What if you lose?" Gia asked.

"I don't intend to lose. But if I do, I'll owe

him something. Don't worry, I'm used to that
sort of thing."

Darren raised an eyebrow as a message flashed
on screen.

Studpuppet: choose your weapons,
scoundrel

Darren looked over at Gia. "What do you
think?"

"Basketball," Gia said. "You can't stump me on
trivia."

Darren went back to the keyboard.

Raspuddin: Hoops and hollers at 20 paces!

Suddenly, the room went black and the music
from the other room faded. Disappointed cries
came from the rest of the frat house.

Gia heard Darren turn in his chair. "I bet
Colonel Mustard blew another fuse," he said.
"I better see if I can help. It *is* supposed to
be my party, after all."

"Uh...okay, I guess," Gia said. She wasn't
thrilled at the thought of being left alone in
the dark.

Gia heard Darren get up from his chair. She
couldn't see anything. She was about to say

that she would come with him when he cried out in surprise.

"Darren?" she called out.

Someone grunted and fell to the floor. Gia heard footsteps retreating, then the door leading out of the computer room swung open.

Just then the lights came back on. Darren was on the floor, clutching his nose. It was bleeding! Then a sheet of paper sitting on the keyboard caught her eye.

Gia, don't forget about OUR date...
D.B.

Gia gasped. "Dethboy..."

3

"Are you all right?" Gia asked, hurrying to Darren's side. He shrugged off her attempts to help him to his feet. Wiping his bloody nose, Darren eyed the typewritten note sitting on the keyboard.

Gia, don't forget about OUR date...
D.B.

"Why didn't you tell me you had a boyfriend?" Darren demanded.

Gia stared at Darren in shock. Then she looked at the note again and understood what Darren meant. He thought he'd just been roughed up by a jealous boyfriend. No wonder he was upset. He had no way of knowing that "D.B." was really Dethboy.

"I don't have a boyfriend!" Gia protested. "It's not what it looks like!"

"Yeah, right," Darren said as he made his way to the door. "Man, I can't believe I stuck up for you."

That startled her. "What are you talking about?" Gia asked as she followed him to the hall.

"Never mind." Darren tore off through the crowd.

"Darren, wait!" Gia said, hurrying behind him. "I can explain—"

Darren wheeled around to face Gia. "You've done enough damage for tonight, all right?" he said loudly. Then he turned and headed upstairs. His outburst caused a sudden silence in the room. Gia realized that everyone was staring at her.

"Start the music," Lee said as he made his way through the crowd.

Colonel Mustard cranked up a new tune. Everyone started dancing. Everyone except Jenny. She seemed startled, confused. It looked like she was about to say something when Lee stepped between Gia and Jenny. "Did Wally find you?" he asked.

Gia's head was spinning. "Wally?"

"He was here, looking for you."

Gia shook her head.

"Why don't you try to scare him up? I'll go upstairs and talk to Darren. See if I can calm him down. What happened, anyway?"

Gia told him. Lee shook his head. "This is bad. You want to call campus security?"

Gia hugged herself. "I think I'll try to find Wally first."

"Okay," Lee said. "Be right back."

Gia watched Lee head up the stairs. She was about to go looking for Wally when she heard someone say his name. Just ahead, two girls were talking about him.

"He bumped right into me!" said a red-haired young woman in a pink sweater. "Can you believe that? I mean, the way Wally Weird ran out of here, you'd think he just killed someone or something!"

"Yeah, and did you see that stuff on his shirt?" her friend asked. "Like he spilled punch all over himself!"

Gia looked at the glasses of punch in everybody's hands. It was red fruit punch. Red…like blood. Suddenly, a terrible thought occurred to her. She'd been on-line with Wally when Dethboy dragged her to his cyberlair. Wally knew enough about computers to pull that off.

Then there was that photo of her roommate, Peggy, that she saw in the lair. Peggy looked as if she had been murdered. Lee said that someone could have faked that with computer graphics. Someone like Wally. And though Wally looked shy, he was on his way to becoming a master at Cuong-Nhu martial arts. He could have roughed up Darren, no problem. And gotten blood on his shirt...

There was no Dethboy. It had been Wally the whole time, playing some kind of twisted joke!

Gia went upstairs looking for Lee and Darren, but they were nowhere to be found. She couldn't wait around any longer. Grabbing her coat, she left the frat house. She had to do something. She had to find Wally and find out what was going on.

Soon she was walking across campus, the sounds of the party fading behind her. There wasn't much of a moon tonight. Several of the lights were out on the quad. It was hard to see where she was going.

She passed a Roman-style building. The main auditorium. A sound came from her right. She turned and saw a shadow dart behind a huge stone column. Gia tensed. "Wally?" she asked, hopefully.

The figure emerged from the shadows. All she could see was a vague outline. "Why are you doing this?" Gia asked. "I thought you were my friend."

The figure came to the top of the stairs. Gia felt a chill that had nothing to do with the cool night air. Now she could see jeans, a pea green winter coat with a hood, and black gloves. There was only darkness inside the hood.

"Say something!" Gia snarled.

"You're beautiful when you're angry."

Gia took a step back. That wasn't Wally's voice. It was too low, too ragged. It barely sounded human.

The figure took another step forward and tossed back his hood. He wore a black wool mask over his face. Slits had been cut for his eyes and mouth. "You got my note, right?" he asked. "I don't know about you, but I never stand up my dates..."

Gia's blood turned to ice. Dethboy! She turned and ran.

"'She walks in Beauty, like the night!'" Dethboy called as he came after her. "'Of cloudless climes and starry skies! And all that's best of dark and bright meet in her aspect and her eyes!'"

Gia was terrified. This guy was out of his mind!

"Hey, come on! That's poetry!" Dethboy cried out. "We're like Romeo and Juliet!"

Gia's heart thundered. She could hear Dethboy gaining on her. She cried out for help, hoping someone would hear. Dethboy laughed.

Suddenly, Gia heard a shrill cry and a grunt of pain. Her instincts told her not to look back, because she might see how close he was.

Gia looked back.

She saw Dethboy sprawled on the ground. It looked like he'd tripped, but now he was starting to get up. Crane Hall was still two blocks away. Gia kept running.

The Shaffer Library loomed up ahead. Once before, she'd come to the library hoping to pull an all-nighter, only to find the windows dark but the door unlocked.

She cut across the quad, away from Crane Hall. There was another dorm past the library. With any luck, Dethboy would think she was going there and try to cut her off. Out of the corner of her eye, she saw Dethboy changing direction. He was falling for the fake-out!

At the last possible second, Gia darted up the front stairs of the library. She heard Dethboy cry out in frustration as she ran to the front door. She turned the knob. It wasn't locked. But the door wasn't opening. It was stuck!

"Gotcha!" Dethboy cried. He was right behind her.

Gia tried the door again, pulling harder this

time. With a groan, the door swung open. Gia
darted inside and threw her weight up against
the door. She reached for the lock and realized it was broken. She ran ahead, slamming
into a long table, then scrambled over the
information desk and crouched down behind it,
waiting.

She heard the door open. The sound of ragged
breathing filled the room. All she could see
was Dethboy's feet. He was coming her way. Gia
tried not to panic. She had to stay calm. She
had to outthink Dethboy.

Okay, she told herself. Where's the last place
he would expect you to go?

It came to her suddenly. The tombs. Where they
stored all the old newspapers. She had been
down there plenty of times. She was pretty
sure that door had a lock on the inside. Even
better, the tombs had only one door in or out.
And no windows. He'd expect her to run *from*
the library, not deeper into it...

Dethboy was getting closer. He turned away for
a moment. Gia looked around for a weapon. She
poked her head up quickly. Resting on the sur-
face of the desk was a heavy blue paperweight
about the size of a baseball. A plan formed in
her mind. Quickly, she grabbed the paperweight
and threw it as hard as she could. It smashed
a glass window a dozen feet to his right.
Dethboy turned, startled.

Gia was already in motion, cutting a path behind him in the other direction. He had fallen for the distraction. Her hand hit the back of a chair and she gasped at the sudden pain. Dethboy whirled at the sound and ran after her.

Gia scrambled down the stairs leading to the tombs, Dethboy right on her heels. He reached out to grab her, but his gloved hand only grazed her jacket. Gia was moving faster than she ever had in her life.

She ran through the open passageway, grabbed hold of the heavy door to the tombs, and tried to slam it shut behind her. But Dethboy blocked it with his weight. Gia felt herself sliding back as he pushed the door open. Then her legs hit something. A heavy desk. It braced her. She shoved back as hard as she could.

Dethboy jammed his leg in the doorway. He reached past the door for her face!

Gia dug her hand into her purse, yanked out her keys, and drove the sharp points down hard on Dethboy's knee. He screamed in pain. She eased the pressure she was putting on the door for just a second, then struck again. Dethboy jumped back. Gia slammed the door shut and turned the lock.

Dethboy pounded at the door in a rage, but she

ignored him. Feeling around in the darkness, she moved the heavy desk against the door. She used everything she could find in the tombs to form an immovable barricade.

There was no way Dethboy could get in. No other doors led into this room and no windows peered out of it. She could wait here until morning, when the library would be crawling with students. Dethboy would be gone by then.

"This isn't over!" Dethboy howled.

"No kidding," Gia whispered. After everything that had happened, it wasn't going to be over until she said it was. She would find out who this guy was and what kind of game he was playing.

Then she was going to bring him down.

4

Gia was jolted awake by a pounding at the door. Fear surged through her. It was Dethboy! He'd come back—and this time he was going to break the door down!

"Is anyone in there?" a woman called. Relief flooded through Gia. "Mrs. Burgess!" she cried out. Gia never thought she'd be so glad to hear the head librarian's stern voice. She checked her watch and saw that it was seven in the morning.

Gia rose, stiff from sleeping on the floor, and started clearing away the pile of furniture in front of the door. Finally, Gia was able to let Mrs. Burgess and her student assistant into the room.

"What were you *doing* in here?" demanded Mrs. Burgess.

Gia gasped as she saw the marks Dethboy had left on the other side of the door while trying to get inside. What had he used? A crowbar? An ax? She didn't want to know.

"I hope you have a good explanation for all this," said Mrs. Burgess as she led Gia upstairs. They entered the main room of the

library, and Gia saw the window she had shattered the night before.

"How did this happen?" Mrs. Burgess demanded.
"And did you have something to do with all the
broken lamps outside?"

"Broken lamps?" Gia replied. Then it struck
her. Dethboy! He'd broken the lights on the
quad, so she wouldn't see him coming!

Gia took a deep breath. "I'm sorry about the
window—" she began.

Mrs. Burgess wasn't listening. "Why don't we
go to campus security," she said, throwing
open the front door. "You can tell them how
sorry you are."

"Fine," Gia said. "Let's go." As she walked
with Mrs. Burgess across campus, Gia studied
the faces of the students they passed. Any one
of them could be Dethboy, she realized. There
was no way of knowing.

They entered the lobby of the security building and were met by a red-haired man in a blue
uniform. "Mrs. Burgess? Brian Donachy," the
man said. "I got a call from your assistant
telling me to expect you. I'll handle Ms. Gibson from here."

The librarian looked pleased. "She admitted
that she broke my window."

"We'll take care of it," Donachy assured her. He turned and walked down a narrow corridor, gesturing for Gia to follow.

Donachy took her to a small office near the rear of the building and pulled a chair out for her. The office's lime green walls were covered with memos and photographs.

The officer sat down and started flipping through a stack of files on his desk. "Why don't you tell me what happened, Ms. Gibson."

"I was coming home from a party," Gia blurted out. "This guy came after me. Jeans, green coat, gloves, a black wool mask. He chased me to the library, and I had to lock myself in the tombs to get away from him. I'm sorry about the window, but I had to do something to distract him—so I could get to the tombs."

Gia waited for some kind of reaction from Donachy, but he seemed much more interested in his files than in her story. Something told her to hold off on telling Donachy about her troubles on-line.

Donachy shrugged. "Actually, I'm glad you're here. Saves me the trouble of bringing you in." He opened the first of the files before him. "Three students have registered com- plaints about you."

Gia thought he must be kidding. "About *me*?"

"Uh-huh," Donachy said. "Phone calls, surprise visits, e-mail threats, torn-up clothing. And that was only the first guy."

"I don't believe this," Gia muttered. "What first guy? I haven't been out with *anyone* since I got to Wintervale!"

"Number two," Donachy said, opening another file. "This guy says you almost got him suspended for cheating on an exam. You planted a cheat sheet on his hard drive and sent the professor an anonymous note about it."

Gia was too stunned to say a word.

Donachy flipped open yet another file. "This one's my favorite. Now this guy—Ted Leonetti—sound familiar?"

Gia stared at him in disbelief. She shook her head.

"Ted says you got on the campus net and convinced everyone, including his girlfriend, that he was cheating on her." Donachy shoved the file in Gia's direction. "With you."

Gia hugged herself. Suddenly, she understood. The strange looks she'd been getting recently, wherever she went. And at the party, Darren had said that he'd stood up for her. It must have been about this. With a sinking feeling, Gia realized that these rumors about her must have been spread across the entire campus. And they must have been spread by Dethboy.

"This is ridiculous," Gia protested. "I've never heard about any of this before. What about the guy who chased me last night?"

Donachy leaned across his desk. "I figure one of these guys you've been messing with got fed up and decided to teach you a lesson."

"I want to talk to these guys," Gia said firmly.

"No way," said Donachy. "I catch you within fifty feet of any of them, and I'll have you suspended. I tried to talk these boys into filing criminal charges, but they're not interested. They just want to be left alone. And one more thing..."

"What's that?" Gia asked, struggling to control her temper.

"I'll be watching you," Donachy said slowly, "so watch your step."

Gia nodded and got to her feet. "That's it?"

"For now."

Gia stalked out of the security building into the bright morning sun. Her stomach growled with hunger, but she was too upset to eat anything.

Just then, someone tapped her on the shoulder. Startled, she turned to face Wally.

"Are you mad at me?" he asked.

Gia had never been so glad to see anyone in her life. "No," she said. She looked deeply into his eyes and wondered how she ever could have doubted him.

"I'm sorry I bagged on you in the chat room last night," Wally said. "When you asked about making a run at the Rat—"

"You don't have to say anything," she said.

"Yeah, I do. I just didn't want to disappoint you," Wally explained. "I can't get into the Rat either. You keep calling me a computer guru and everything—"

"Which you are," Gia said. It was kind of nice, in an odd way, to comfort someone else. It took her mind off how badly *she* needed to be comforted.

"I was talking to my roommate about what happened," Wally went on. "Peter said I was acting stupid, and I just wanted to say I was sorry. I went to that party looking for you, but I couldn't find you."

Gia almost started to cry. She threw her arms around Wally's neck and held on tight. Wally looked around uncomfortably. Once she started speaking, it all came out in a mad rush. Gia told Wally about Dethboy, the incident at the party, and the encounter in the library. Wally cut her off before she could tell him about her run-in with Donachy.

"Come on," he said. "I've got an idea."

Gia followed Wally back to Crane Hall. She practically had to run after him—he was on a mission. Wally booted up Gia's computer and started searching various directories.

"What are you looking for?" Gia asked.

"Every time you visit a Web site, the computer stores the information," Wally said, his fingers jamming on the keyboard. "I think I can follow the route you took and get us to Dethboy's site."

He made some notes on a piece of paper, then called up the campus net. Gia entered her password and logged on. Wally took it from there. Five minutes later, they were hopping from one home page to another. "Does any of this look familiar?" Wally asked.

Gia shrugged. "I don't know. It all went by so fast."

Wally keyed in a few more codes, and suddenly the screen went black. Gia grabbed the back of Wally's arm, her nails digging into his flesh. She was terrified of seeing the photo of

Peggy's body again.

But instead, a rabbit hopped across the screen.
It had Wally's face, and it carried a sign.

THIS WAY TO WALLY WORLD!

Gia couldn't believe what she was seeing.
Wally looked stunned. He clicked on the rabbit. A few seconds later, a graphic came up of
an amusement park.

WALLY WORLD!

Home of Wintervale's answer to
Revenge of the Nerds—Wally Deitz!

"Turn it off," Gia said, but Wally ignored
her.

Instead, he clicked on his name, and a whole
page came up of nasty nicknames that people
called him.

Danger Deitz
Walla Walla Wally
Wally Weird

At the bottom of the screen, a banner read,

Presented by Ripley!

Wally backed away from the computer, aston-
ished. A small graphic popped up.

"Wait a minute," Gia said. "I didn't do this. Think about it, Wally. I wouldn't even know how."

He wouldn't look at her. "Your buddies over at the frat house would."

"YOU HAVE MAIL!" chimed a voice from the computer.

"Better get that," Wally said, heading out the door.

Gia ran after him. "No, Wally! Wait!" But when she got to the hall, he was gone.

Gia went back to her computer and clicked on the little mailbox. A letter came through from a screen name she didn't recognize: Goldeneye.

> Gia, I know what's going on. I can help you. Meet me in the bell tower at four o'clock.
>
> —Adrian

Gia stared at the note. She knew that Adrian could very well be Dethboy. It could be a trap. The old bell tower was closed for repairs. It was dangerous in there, but she had to do something. She sent back a reply.

Ripley: See you there…

5

Gia stood on the bell tower's fifth-story landing and peered out the window, her heart racing. Adrian had said to meet here at four. Now it was five minutes past, and no one was approaching the tower. She didn't know how much longer she could take this. The waiting was killing her.

Clutching her bottle of Diet Coke, Gia glanced up at the massive bells looming over her. Then she looked across the makeshift bridge toward the opposite landing. There was another stair-well on that side of the tower. Maybe Adrian was coming up that way. The bridge connecting the two landings under the bells had been dis-mantled. There was no railing and only a wood-en plank spanned the gap. No wonder the tower was off-limits.

This is crazy, she thought. Coming up here alone was a big mistake. She'd wanted Wally or Lee to come with her, but couldn't find either of them. If Adrian was Dethboy, then she was walking into a trap...

Suddenly, the bells started ringing. It was deafening. Gia covered her ears with her hands. Before her, a dark figure suddenly appeared. He reached for her! Gia took a step

back. Her feet were on the edge of the landing. She tried to shift her weight, but it was
too late.

Gia screamed as she fell from the landing. The
soda bottle flew from her hand as she reached
out blindly. Her fingers caught on something—
the wooden plank. She clutched at it and hung
in midair. Five stories down, the soda bottle
clattered on the pavement.

Gia looked up at the near landing and saw a
familiar figure. A pea green hooded coat,
a face covered by a black wool mask. Slowly he
kneeled on the landing and held out his hand
to her. Sunlight glinted off something around
his neck. It looked metallic.

"Gia!" came another voice. She turned her head
and saw a dark-haired man appear above her on
the far landing.

"Straus! Don't do anything stupid," Dethboy
said in his low, unearthly voice. Then he
turned back to Gia. "I'm closer than he is.
Take my hand."

"Gia, don't do it!" the other man called. His
voice was deep, and he had an accent. Gia
realized it must be Adrian. "Hold on!" he
shouted.

Adrian stripped off his belt, securing one end
around a support beam and the other around his

ankle. He lay down and reached toward Gia, the upper half of his body stretched out over empty air.

Gia felt herself slipping. In an instant, she made a decision. She grabbed for Adrian's hand as she lost her grip on the wooden board. He caught her! Gia screamed as her body slammed into the far wall. Below her, she could hear the wooden board banging against the walls as it plummeted to the ground.

Adrian grunted as he tried to pull Gia up.

"Hurry!" Dethboy yelled. "The belt is coming open!"

Gia cried out as Adrian slipped down a couple of inches, then jerked to a stop. With a groan, he hauled her over the edge of the landing, just as the belt came undone.

Gasping, Gia looked over to the opposite landing. Dethboy was gone. His echoing voice rose from the stairwell. "Good to see you again, Straus. I'll tell Rebecca you said hi…"

Adrian shook his head. "Unbelievable," he muttered.

Gia could hear voices outside. She got up and looked out the window. People were coming to the tower to investigate why the bells had rung.

Adrian grabbed Gia's hand. "Let's get out of here."

They made their way back down the stairwell. By the time they reached the ground, Dethboy was nowhere to be found.

"Come on," Adrian said, leading Gia away from the approaching crowd to a trail that skirted the edge of the woods. "I'm sorry about what happened. I didn't want Dethboy to know I was helping you. That's why I wanted to meet in the bell tower. But he must have followed you. Now we're gonna have to think of something else."

Gia stopped suddenly. "Wait a minute," she said. "I'm grateful for what you did back there, but who are you, and what's going on?"

Adrian looked at her for a long moment. "I'll tell you," he said. "But not here. I know a place."

Ten minutes later, they were sitting in a darkened lecture hall. An old black-and-white movie was playing. They slid into seats near the back of the room. Adrian sat with his back against the wall, keeping an eye on the exits. A handful of students sat near the front.

Gia watched a woman on screen walk down a shadowy corridor that seemed to come alive.

"Jean Cocteau's *Beauty and the Beast*," Adrian said. "Pretty surreal."

Gia nodded. "So what's the deal, Adrian?"

"All right," Adrian said, keeping his voice low. "A year ago, I was a freshman here, just like you. If you're wondering about my accent, I'm from Austria. I had a girlfriend. Her name was—"

"Rebecca," Gia said. "Dethboy said her name."

Adrian flinched. "Yeah. Rebecca. She and I were doing great. Then Dethboy started turning everyone against her, including me. By the time I realized that her stories about this guy who was terrorizing her on-line were true, it was too late. Rebecca disappeared a year ago this Friday."

"How'd you know about me and Dethboy?" Gia asked.

"I was at Darren's party last night," Adrian explained. "When I was upstairs, I overheard your friend Lee talking to Darren. He told Darren about your visit to Dethboy's site and the picture of Peggy. Darren said something about a note from D.B., and Lee said it had to be Dethboy. That's when I knew that what had happened to Rebecca was happening to you."

Gia realized her hands were trembling. Adrian reached over in the darkness and put his hands

over hers. She looked over at him. She hadn't
realized how good-looking he was until this
moment.

"It'll be all right," Adrian said, releasing
her hands awkwardly.

"What did Darren say when Lee told him?"

Adrian looked away. "Darren didn't buy a word
of it, and before too long, he had Lee doubting it, too. There are stories going around
about you—"

"I know," Gia said. She told Adrian about her
encounter with Donachy at campus security. But
something else was gnawing at her. "If Dethboy
wanted to get rid of me, why didn't he just
kick at the board? That's all he had to do. He
was acting like he didn't want me to get
hurt."

"He's a control freak," Adrian said. "The way
I figure it, he doesn't want anything happening to you until he's good and ready."

Gia nodded, but she had a strange feeling that
there was more to it than that. A lot more.

"Look," Adrian said. "I've been trying to fig-
ure out what this guy's been up to for a year.
I've got some ideas. I saw his lair once, and
I think I know where to find it again."

Gia leaned forward. "Where?" she asked.

"The Rat. I think it's a secret room way off the Rat. But you have to get in there first."

Gia shook her head. "I've only been in there with Darren. He was using program keys, so I didn't see the passwords."

"If you can get to that computer," said Adrian, "bring it to a DOS prompt and hit those program keys. It'll show the codes. All you have to do is print them out. With those passwords, you'll be able to get into the Rat."

Gia nodded slowly. "That sounds good," she said.

"I'm also thinking that we should try to get that note Dethboy left for you. It's evidence that all this isn't just in your head. And I want to check out those guys who filed complaints about you. See if I can find out who put them up to it."

"All right," Gia said. "Great. So what do we do first?"

"*We're* not doing anything," Adrian said, avoiding her gaze. "You're going to have to do this on your own."

"But Dethboy's out there—"

"Don't worry about him. Now that he knows I'm involved, he's going to want to get rid of me.

I'm going to give him every opportunity to do that. I'll keep him distracted so he doesn't have time to go after you. Besides, if I know anything about Dethboy, you're safe until Friday."

"The same day Rebecca disappeared."

Adrian nodded.

"How am I gonna know if you're okay or not?" Gia asked.

"I'll hook up with you on-line. Goldeneye, remember?"

"Yeah. And your last name is Straus. Adrian Straus."

He frowned. "Don't push it. I'll see you later." With that, he got up and left her in the darkness.

* * *

Back in his room, Adrian booted up his computer and logged on to the campus net. It didn't take long before his faceless partner found him. It never did. Adrian reported everything that had happened that night. He thought for a moment, then added:

Goldeneye: I did what you wanted. You're sure this will work?

Q: I want Dethboy as much as you do. He's broken the rules. Nobody acts in the real world unless I say they do.

Goldeneye: I don't feel right about using Gia like this.

Q: Nothing will happen to Gia. I want her safe as much as you do. Even more so.

Goldeneye: Why?

Q: I have my reasons. Don't question them.

The connection went dead. Adrian turned off his computer. Q. Very clever. The guy who outfitted James Bond with all his gadgets. But Adrian didn't care what this guy called himself.

Adrian thought of him as the Lurker.

6

Gia sneaked in the back door of the frat house. She figured if anyone stopped her, she'd say she was looking for Darren. Which wasn't far from the truth anyway. She needed to set things straight.

It was dark, and the light was off in the hall. She wanted to find that note Dethboy had left. *And* she had to get the codes for the Rat from Darren's computer if she was going to return to Dethboy's lair.

Heading down the hall, she came to an open doorway. It was the kitchen. No one was in there. Suddenly, she heard voices. She ducked into the kitchen as a pair of frat guys walked by. They stopped just outside.

"Man, I can't believe it's already time for exams," one of the guys said.

"Tell me about it," said the other guy.

Glancing around the kitchen, Gia noticed another door at the far end of the room. It was half open, with blue light flickering through. Gia took a deep breath and crept toward it, hoping no one was in there.

Gia peered into the darkened room. A bunch of guys sat on the couch and floor watching a video of the party. On the screen, Colonel Mustard was rocking. The frat guys howled with laughter as they watched Lee dancing wildly.

Gia was wondering how she would get to the computer room without the guys seeing her, when suddenly she heard voices behind her.

"You want a soda?"

"Sure…"

Gia couldn't believe it. The two guys from outside the kitchen were coming her way. She was trapped!

Suddenly, one of the guys in the living room went over to the window and hooted, "Dudes! Check this out!" He opened the window and yelled, "Yo, Jenny! Lookin' good!" Everyone clambered over themselves to catch a glimpse of Jenny.

Gia saw that their backs were turned to her… Now was her chance. She slipped into the living room, behind the guys. As she darted down the adjoining corridor, an image flashed into Gia's mind: Jenny in one of her cute little dresses, loving all the attention.

One of the guys started jumping up and down. "Hey, Jenny's coming this way!"

Gia sneaked down the corridor to the computer room. She knew she didn't have much time. She'd have to work fast. She reached for the doorknob, then froze. It was already starting to turn!

Gia darted into the closet across the hall and hid under a pile of wrinkled jerseys. Through a crack in the door, she watched a couple of guys leave the computer room and head down the hall.

Gia left her hiding place. She opened the door to the computer room slowly and peered inside. It was empty. Perfect.

"About that dress." Gia jumped at the sound of a voice right next to her. It was Jenny!

Jenny gave Gia a smile, then brushed past her into the computer room. "Come on," Jenny said. "I dropped an earring in here."

Without a word, Gia followed Jenny inside and shut the door.

Jenny began looking around the room. "I just want you to know that it's cool between us. The dress was no big deal, okay?"

"I wasn't trying to show you up," Gia said.

"Like you could," Jenny shot back as she knelt down near one of the computers. She stood up with a jade earring in her hand. "That's not what I wanted to talk to you about anyway. I know you're in trouble. Lee told me everything."

Gia shook her head in disbelief. "Might as well just put it in the student newspaper," she muttered.

"Lee's your friend," said Jenny. "And as hard as it may be for you to believe, I'm trying to be your friend, too. So take the advice of someone who knows what you're going through. Leave Wintervale. Now. Don't even bother packing. Just go."

"You can't be serious."

"I am. You can't win. It's impossible. There are a lot of schools out there. Your problems aren't going to follow you. It's about this place." She paused and glanced at the door. "*He* doesn't leave Wintervale. If you go, you'll be safe. I wish I had."

"Wait a minute," Gia said. "Are you telling me you know who Dethboy is?"

Before Jenny could say another word, the door swung open. The guys who'd been in the computer room earlier stopped in their tracks when they saw Gia there with Jenny.

"Hey, Jenny," said one of the guys. "What are you doing with that loser?"

Jenny glared at them. "Wasting time. You guys know all about that, don't you?" Then she flipped her hair over her shoulder and stormed out.

The guys looked at Gia as if she were a bug they wouldn't mind squashing. "You found the door the other night," one of them said. "Find it again."

Gia hurried out of the frat house and made a beeline for Crane Hall. Back in her dorm room, Gia booted up her computer and checked her mail. Adrian had just left a message, instructing her to join him in a private chat room. She was there in a flash.

> **Ripley:** I didn't get the codes or the note. I blew it.:(
> **Goldeneye:** Can you go back?
> **Ripley:** No way. Got major league busted—not that Jenny helped any
> **Goldeneye:** Jenny Dvorak?
> **Ripley:** yeah, the ice princess. She said she knows who DB is, but I don't buy it. And she told me I should leave Wintervale
> **Goldeneye:** Maybe you should...

Gia couldn't believe what Adrian was saying.

> **Ripley:** I've worked too hard to get here!!! No way am I quitting. I still don't know if Peggy's all right...and I thought you wanted to find out about Rebecca

It seemed like forever before Adrian wrote
back.

> **Goldeneye:** I know, I'm sorry. It's just…I
> don't want you to get hurt. It was nice
> being with you today. The movie part, I
> mean…Maybe we could do something like
> that again?

Gia sat back in surprise. She smiled—the
offer was flattering. But it was Darren she
had the crush on. Not Adrian. Still, the feel
of Adrian's hands on hers…

> **Ripley:** can't talk about that now. Gotta
> come up with another plan for getting the
> codes!
> **Goldeneye:** No problem. Check this out!

Suddenly, an array of codes flashed across
Gia's screen.

> **Ripley:** how'd you get those?!!!!
> **Goldeneye:** I've been working on this guy
> for a while, trying to get him to sell me
> his codes. Tonight he came to me. I would
> have tried to head you off at the frat,
> but it was too late
> **Ripley:** That's okay. There was still a
> chance I would have found Dethboy's note.
> **Goldeneye:** So, what d'ya say…you up for a
> run at the Rat?

Gia was psyched at the idea. Then she heard a
knock at the door. "Yeah?!"

"Someone's on the phone for you!" called
Marissa Valero, the floor R.A.

"Who is it?" asked Gia. "I'm busy."

"The connection's pretty bad, but I think it's
Peggy."

Gia was shocked. If it really was Peggy, if
her roommate was alive…

Gia turned back to her keyboard.

> **Ripley:** BBL
> **Goldeneye:** take your time…

*   *   *

In a darkened room, the Lurker typed one more
line before signing off.

> **Goldeneye:** I'll be here.

Jenny Dvorak's betrayal was disappointing.
There would be consequences. Otherwise,
tonight was going according to plan. The
deal with Adrian Straus was working out well.
Adrian handled Gia in the real world. But on-
line, Gia belonged entirely to the Lurker.

Well, maybe not entirely. Not yet.

But soon…

7

Gia raced to the pay phone at the end of the hall, and Marissa followed. Gia couldn't believe how much her hand was trembling as she picked up the receiver.

"Peg?" Gia asked, praying that her missing roommate was okay. At first, all she heard was a hailstorm of static. Then came a familiar voice.

"Hey, Poodle Head."

Gia's heart thundered. It was Peggy! That meant the photo she'd seen yesterday in Deth-boy's lair was a fake. Her roommate was alive!

"Peg, where—"

The static came again. "I've only got a second, you better let me do the talking."

"Okay," Gia said, blinking back tears of relief. "But—"

"I'm gonna be tied up for a while," Peggy said in a small voice. She sounded upset. Even a little frightened.

"Peg?" Gia said.

The voice on the other end of the phone continued as if Gia weren't even there. "We're
gonna be together Friday—"

"Peg, are you all right? Is someone there with
you?"

"—and it'll be lots of fun, like a party—"

"You're really starting to scare me, Peggy."

"—you just gotta promise me you'll be there,
promise—"

Suddenly, Gia heard a muffled voice in the
background. There was another burst of static,
followed by an electronic clicking. Then the
line went dead.

"Peggy!" Gia cried. The only response was a
dial tone. Shaken, Gia hung up the phone. She
turned and slumped against the wall.

Marissa placed a reassuring hand on Gia's
shoulder. "So it was Peggy," Marissa said.

Gia nodded. "Yeah, it's just…I dunno. It was
weird. I was talking, but she didn't seem to
hear me."

"Same thing happened to me," Marissa put in.
"I picked up the phone, and all she said was,
'Gia Gibson, please.' I tried talking to her,
but she just kept saying the same thing over
and over."

Gia felt a sudden chill. Could it have been a recording? An image leaped into her head: Peggy as Dethboy's prisoner, forced to say words that had been written for her.

No, that was crazy. Wasn't it?

"On the other hand, there was a lot of static," Marissa added. "Maybe she just couldn't hear us too well." She paused a moment, then continued. "You know, it's all over campus about her running off with that guy Troy. Did she say anything about him?"

"No, she didn't," Gia said.

How did everyone know about Peggy? Gia wondered. Then she remembered that Peggy's e-mail had come to Jenny by mistake. Jenny must have told everyone. That's why no one was worried about Peggy.

No one except Gia—she was the only one who'd seen the photo of Peggy in Dethboy's lair.

"I gotta go," Gia said, suddenly thinking about Adrian. She really wanted to get back to him and make a run at the Rat. Now more than ever, she had to find Dethboy's lair.

"Just one thing," Marissa said. "I heard about the trouble you're in. I just want you to know that I don't believe any of the things that are being said about you. If you need me, I'm here."

Gia smiled gratefully. "Thanks."

Gia returned to her room and sat down at her computer.

Ripley: are you there?
Goldeneye: yeah—what's going on?

Gia quickly explained what had happened.

Ripley: What I don't understand is what she meant about Friday. She wanted me to be somewhere, but she didn't say where.
Goldeneye: Friday. The day Rebecca disappeared
Ripley: Why are you so sure Dethboy's going to wait until Friday before coming after me again?
Goldeneye: it's all happening the same way, right to the day. Rebecca told me about Dethboy pulling her into his lair on a Sunday, same as you. He came after her that night, but she got away from him, just like you. Then on Monday, a year ago today, I found out she was stalking these guys
Ripley: What happened to Rebecca on Tuesday?
Goldeneye: I don't know. Rebecca and I didn't talk again until that Friday when she disappeared.

Gia leaned back and ran her hands through her hair. It was weird. Why was Adrian the only

one on campus making the connection between
her and Rebecca?

Gia desperately wanted to trust Adrian. He'd
saved her life in the tower. But then, Dethboy
had tried to save her life, too.

There was only one place to find the answer.

> **Ripley:** Let's take that run at the Rat.
> Dethboy's lair must be there
> **Goldeneye:** you go. And make sure you pick
> a new screen name. I'm going to try to
> find those guys who complained about you.
> **Ripley:** Okay. Ciao

Gia printed out the codes Adrian had given
her. The thought of entering the Rat on her
own was exciting. But first, she had to pick a
new screen name, something that would really
obscure her identity, maybe even make her
sound like a guy. She picked a cool name she'd
seen somewhere before.

Night Beest

Gia typed in the codes that would take her
past the Gatekeeper and into the Rat itself.
Part of her wanted to stop at the Hole in the
Wall. It'd be good to pay back the Gatekeeper
for all the put-downs she'd endured...

But no time for that now. Gia launched herself
into the Rat. She zipped past the Gatekeeper

screen and found herself in one of the Rat's
main rooms.

> **Darkling:** Bond, I sincerely hope if you
> wish to play so very bold, you can back
> up your boasts.
> **Bond:** Don't mess with the best, Darkling,
> old chap...after all "Nobody does it bet-
> ter" than 007...You made the wrong enemy
> this time my friend...
> **Red Sonia:** Testing 1, 2...Hello? This is
> Bellevue paging Bond. James Bond.
> **blondie:** anyone seen dagwood???
> **TwiliZone:** curiouser and curiouser
> **Dana Scully:** just because I'm paranoid
> doesn't mean they're not out to get me
> and all of us
> **Scarlet:** oh, James, dear, don't forget
> about me
> **Bond:** frankly, Scarlet
> **Agent Cooper:** The owls are not what they
> seem...

Gia grinned, then switched to another room.

> **Rammer:** I'm the number one RAT!!!
> **Pundit:** Someone's Lurkin over my shoulder
> **Vedder Cheddar:** check it out Raspuddin
> and Studpuppet next door

Raspuddin! Gia couldn't resist checking in on
Darren. She switched to the next room.

> **Studpuppet:** you wimped out, puddinhead

Lord Myron: Mad Monk of the Rat, hmmmmmmm?
Raspuddin: look puppetbreath, I chal-
lenged you to help someone get on the
paper. But I'm not into it anymore—she
turned out to be a psycho

Gia flinched. She couldn't believe this! And
she'd thought Darren was such a great guy. Her
fingers flew across the keys in anger.

Night Beest: a deal's a deal, don't be a
wuss!
Studpuppet: good one, newbie!
Lord Myron: reneging on a duel is not a
gentlemanly thing to do, Raspuddin, no
matter what the reason
Raspuddin: hey, Myron, I hate to break it
to you, but Lord Byron's history. You go
up against me, you're gonna be history,
too
Lord Myron: "Thy innocence and mine to
save, I bid thee now a last farewell!"
Raspuddin: you, too, Night Beest. Go
fight the X-Men or something

Gia was about to reply when it hit her. Lord
Myron was obsessed with Byron. And Dethboy was
into Byron, too! She'd never forget the words
he'd called out to her as he'd chased her
across campus: "She walks in Beauty, like the
night…"

Quickly, Gia started searching for Lord Myron,
leaping from one room to the next. But he
seemed to have vanished.

Gia entered a room and was surprised to find people speaking Japanese. Last night, when she and Darren had been in the Rat, they'd seen the same Japanese word over and over. Now something told her to type it in.

Night Beest: Meinichi

Suddenly, all conversation in the room stopped. Gia wondered what she'd just said. She was about to leave the room when a sentence with her new screen name in it popped up. She couldn't understand a word of it.

Wally's roommate, Peter, was Japanese. The only word he'd taught her in his native language was "yes." She typed it in.

Night Beest: Hai

Several screen names vanished from the small box listing who was in the room. Gia was left alone with one other person. Penndragon. Another computer code flashed before her. She printed out the page, then keyed in the code.

Suddenly, Gia found herself in a private room. The people from the first room had all come here. She recognized their screen names.

Penndragon: How did you learn about the Fraternity?

Gia frowned. The Fraternity? What was that supposed to be? Before she could think of a response, Penndragon spoke again.

   Penndragon: What do you hope to find
   here?

Frustrated, Gia decided to go for broke.

   Night Beest: Dethboy

There was a pause, then a final message.

   Penndragon: This room. Tomorrow at nine.

Gia was suddenly hurled out of the Rat. The
next thing she knew, the computer called out,
"YOU HAVE MAIL!"

Clicking on the icon to open her mail, Gia
wondered about the Fraternity. Penndragon
couldn't have meant a regular campus fraternity. This was something secret, something to
do with Dethboy.

Suddenly, someone pounded on Gia's door.

"Fire!" Marissa shouted. "Get out! Now!"

Gia was about to turn off her computer when
the e-mail opened.

   Beaker: Gia, help! I'm trapped in my
   room!

It was Wally! Gia grabbed her printouts, then
raced to help her friend.

8

The hallway was flooded with panicked students. Gia fought against the steady rush of people attempting to escape the burning dorm. She could smell the fire now. Heat radiated down from the ceiling. The fire was on the second floor—where Wally was trapped!

Suddenly, somebody grabbed Gia. She looked up into the face of a guy she didn't recognize. His long brown hair was slicked back, and he wore two earrings. His eyes were dark and intense. "Come on, Gia, you gotta get outa here!"

Gia stared at him in confusion. He knew her, but she had no idea who he was.

"A friend of mine's up there!" she said.

She pulled away from the guy and watched as he was swallowed up by the crowd. She turned and ran for the stairs.

Gia reached the second floor of Crane Hall and saw flames at the far end of the corridor. Wally's room hadn't been engulfed. Yet. She threw open the door and darted inside.

Wally wasn't there. Neither was Peter. She was about to turn and leave when something caught

her eye: A metal box attached to a black Vel-
cro strap sat beside Wally's computer. Gia
picked it up. The box looked familiar for some
reason. It was small and lightweight. She
dropped it in the pocket of her baggy jeans,
then placed her palm against Wally's computer
monitor.

It was cold. The machine hadn't recently been
used. The e-mail couldn't have come from
Wally—it was a fake!

Gia heard the door slam shut behind her. She
spun around to find Lee pressed up against the
door. "The fire's spreading!" he shouted.
"We're trapped!"

"What are you doing here?" Gia asked.

"I heard about the fire from the guys at the
frat. I was worried about you and Wally."

Gia moved past him and yanked open the door. A
wall of heat forced her back into the room.
Roaring flames filled the hall.

"What are you, crazy?" Lee demanded, slamming
the door shut.

Gia looked around desperately. "The window!"
she cried. She ran over and tried to pry it
open, but it was jammed. Lee came over to
help, but the window wouldn't budge.

"Stand back," Lee said. He picked up Wally's

chair and smashed the window. Gia rushed forward and peered down at the crowd below.

Dozens of students had gathered. When they saw Gia at the window, they raised their arms and called, "Jump! Jump!"

"What a bunch of sickos," Lee said. "They *want* us to jump!"

"They'll catch us," Gia said. "Come on!"

"You gotta be kidding," Lee said. Suddenly, a groaning came from the doorway. Wally's door was starting to buckle!

Gia ran to Wally's bed and tore the sheet away. She draped it over the shards of glass in the window and threw her legs over the frame.

"No way," Lee said.

Taking a deep breath, Gia flung herself from the window. A moment later, hands were on her, catching her, slowing her fall. She opened her eyes and saw the faces of fellow students as they passed her back through the crowd, then set her down.

"Do it!" someone called up to Lee.

Gia watched Lee climb onto the window ledge. The next moment, Lee closed his eyes and jumped. He plummeted like a stone. The crowd caught him, half a dozen students going down in a heap as they broke his fall. Lee rolled off the pile of moaning students and hopped to his feet.

"That was fun!" he cried, joining Gia. They turned and watched smoke billowing out of Crane Hall's second-story windows. A pair of fire trucks pulled up in front of the building as campus security moved the crowd back.

"What were you doing up there, anyway?" Lee asked.

"I got an e-mail from Wally. He said he was trapped in his room."

Lee turned away from her in frustration. "Yeah, right. Then where was he? I can't believe you're starting this again."

"Listen, Lee, everything I've told you is true," Gia said. "There *is* someone after me. And I know what Darren told you at the party last night, but I've never even met those guys who said I was stalking them."

"I want to believe you," Lee said slowly.

"Well, you don't act like it."

Lee ran his hands through his hair. He looked at the fire. Hoses were being turned on the flames. "What do you want me to say? Don't you realize how all this sounds? First you tell me about a photo of Peggy's body. But then she sends an e-mail saying she's fine. You're alone with Darren for ten minutes, and the lights go out. When they come back on, some-one's clocked him."

"I didn't—"

Lee wasn't going to let her finish. "Wally told me your story about some crazy guy in a mask chasing you all over campus. He told me about Wally World, too. That was *really* nice."

"I didn't do any of it! Don't you get it? I'm being set up!"

Lee shook his head. "It's just tough for me to buy all this when you're the only one who's ever seen this DethBozo."

"I'm not the only one who's seen him!" she shouted. "Rebecca saw him, too, and no one believed her until it was too late!"

Lee frowned. "Who's Rebecca?"

Gia realized she'd made a mistake. She'd said too much. But at least she'd stopped herself before mentioning Adrian's name. She wanted what they were doing to stay a secret.

"Dethboy went after her last year," Gia explained. "It started for her on a Sunday, just like me. The next day she was accused of stalking all these guys—same deal as me. A year ago this Friday, she disappeared."

Gia shivered and crossed her arms. "I think that's when Dethboy's coming for me."

Lee shook his head. "I was here last year, and I don't remember anything about this girl Rebecca. How'd you hear about this, anyway?"

Before she could answer, Lee pointed to her pocket and said, "Hey, what's that?"

Gia looked down. One end of the metal box was sticking out of her jeans. "I don't know," she said, pulling it out. "I found it in Wally's room." She handed him the box.

Lee turned it over in his hands. "I know what this is," he said. "See these little holes? It's like a speaker. Listen." He put the box against his throat and whispered, "*I'm coming to get you, Gia!*"

The voice that came out was cold and metallic. Unearthly.

Dethboy's voice!

Gia backed away. Lee handed her the box. "You try it," he said.

With trembling hands, Gia put the box against her throat. "*T-testing—*" she whispered.

The same voice came out. With a start, Gia dropped the box to the ground. Lee scooped it up. "My uncle had throat surgery," he explained. "Afterward, he wore something like this." Lee strapped the box around his throat.

"Don't!" Gia said. "It creeps me out."

Lee lowered the box. "What's the matter?" he asked.

Gia suddenly remembered why the metal box looked so familiar. "I was in the bell tower yesterday—"

"That was *you* ringing the bells?" Lee asked, rolling his eyes. "It drove Donachy crazy."

"Just listen to me," Gia said. "It was Dethboy. He was there, too. I saw something shiny, like metal, around his neck." She snatched the voice-altering device back from Lee and placed it against her throat. "*And this is what he sounded like!*"

Lee didn't look convinced. "Uh-huh..."

"I didn't think Dethboy was Wally, because it didn't sound like him," said Gia. "But with one of these—"

"Anyone would sound like Dethboy," Lee finished. "So—now you think it's Wally?"

"No," Gia said, shaking her head. "Someone

wants me to think it's Wally." An image popped into her head of the long-haired guy who'd grabbed her in the hall. "I'm saying Dethboy could be anyone. It could even be more than one person."

Yeah, she thought. Like a whole *Fraternity* of them.

"All right," Lee said. "I'm not saying I believe you, and I'm not saying I don't." He held out his hand. "Let me hold on to the box."

"Why?" Gia asked.

"I want to show it to Wally," said Lee. "See if he knows anything about it. I'll ask Peter, too."

Gia hesitated for a moment. She wanted badly to win back Lee's trust. He was probably the one person on campus she could depend on. And Wally and Peter might open up to him…

She handed over the box.

Marissa walked up as Lee slipped the box into his pocket. "Lee, we could use some help set-ting up the gym. Most of Crane Hall will be spending the night there," she said, nodding at the crowd.

"No problem," Lee said. He looked over at Gia. "You coming?"

"Sure."

They walked over to the gym. Lee went to set up beds. Gia looked around and wondered how she could help out. The room was becoming crowded as students wandered in for the night.

Gia turned and walked right into a woman carrying an overflowing punch bowl. Fruit punch splashed all over her. Gia looked down. She was soaked!

The woman apologized over and over, but Gia barely noticed. All she could think about were the printouts from her run at the Rat earlier that night. She pulled the folded sheets out of her pocket and sat down to look at them. Her baggy sweatshirt and thick jeans had protected the pages. They were a little wet, but all the Japanese words could still be read.

"Do you believe in the Silence?" a voice said behind her.

Gia whirled in her chair. Peter was standing right behind her. He was handsome, with a runner's body, lean and muscular. He smiled, but his eyes were cold.

Peter pointed at the printout. With a shudder, Gia realized he'd quietly been reading over her shoulder. "That's what they asked you," Peter told her. "Do you believe in the Silence? With Silence capitalized, a very important word. And before that, they're plan-

ning to go to a secret place, to make prepara-
tions for a big party."

"Um—" Gia said.

"Meinichi," Peter said. "You know what that
means, don't you?"

Gia was on her feet, heading toward the girls'
locker room. "I gotta dry myself off, I, uh—"

"Death Day. That's what it means. Strange,
isn't it?" Smiling, Peter walked away, leaving
Gia feeling very, very alone.

9

Early Tuesday morning, Gia walked back to
Crane Hall. She squinted against the sun's
harsh glare. The cold morning air made her
shiver. And she couldn't stop yawning—she'd
been too wired to get much sleep last night at
the gym.

As she passed a small group of students, she
caught bits and pieces of their conversation.

"They're throwing the switch tonight! KLRK
rocks!"

"Have you seen Val, the deejay? She's hot!"

"About time Wintervale got its own college
radio station…"

Gia tuned them out. She wished she could just
sit back and enjoy life at school like her
classmates. But she had other things to worry
about.

Like survival.

Gia turned a corner and saw Crane Hall for the
first time since the fire. Several second-
floor windows were charred black holes. A
nasty smell drifted toward her.

"Home sweet dorm," Gia muttered. She was glad she was allowed to return to her first-floor room. The second floor would be off-limits for a while.

Stepping into her room, Gia was relieved to find her stuff pretty much as she'd left it. Her clothes smelled like smoke, but a trip to the laundry room would take care of that. She booted up her computer and was glad to find an e-mail from Adrian.

To: Ripley
From: Goldeneye

Dear Princess Gia,
I hope the Force is with you—I could use some of it right now. I'm going climbing with those three guys who accused you of stalking them. Surprise, surprise—it turns out they know each other. We're heading out this morning. Did I mention I'm scared of heights? You probably couldn't tell at the bell tower. Just goes to show what I'm willing to do for you.

Anyway, I saw you in the gym last night. I wanted to talk to you, but you'd conked out, and I figured you needed the rest. I'm anxious to find out what happened on your run last night, but don't e-mail me back. I don't know how safe it is. Be back soon!

Ciao, U No Who

Gia sighed. She wished Adrian were here, so that she could tell him about the Fraternity—and Death Day. Even though Peter had translated her Japanese printouts from the Rat last night, she had no reason to trust him. She had to go to the library anyway that morning. She'd double-check Peter's translation while she was there.

But first, Gia had some unfinished—and unpleasant—business to take care of.

She went to the phone and dialed Peggy's home number. Mrs. Parrish answered on the third ring. "Hello?"

"Mrs. Parrish? This is Gia Gibson, Peggy's roommate."

"Oh," said Mrs. Parrish. "Hi, Gia. I didn't expect to hear from you."

Gia took a deep breath. "Mrs. Parrish, I need to talk to you about Peggy—"

"Did you know she was going to do it?" Mrs. Parrish interrupted.

Gia was startled. "What?"

"I just can't believe her, running off with this Troy person. Getting married without telling us…"

Gia's heart started to race. "You heard from Peggy?"

"I got a note in the mail," Mrs. Parrish said sadly. "Peg didn't even call."

Gia slumped in her chair. "Was there a return address?"

"No. But it was postmarked somewhere in Texas. It was strange, she didn't even sign it."

"What do you mean?" Gia asked.

"Her letter was typed."

Gia sat up straight. A typewritten note! Just like the one Dethboy had left in the frat computer room.

Gia told Mrs. Parrish a little about the call she'd received from Peggy the night before.

"So she'll be back at school Friday?" Mrs. Parrish asked. "Well, you tell my daughter to call me the second she gets there. I'd like to have a little talk with her…"

"I'll bet," Gia said. "Look, could I ask a favor? Could you send me that letter by overnight mail?"

"Sure, but—"

Gia tapped the hold button on her handset.

"Oh, I just got another call. I should run. Thanks!"

Gia hung up. She didn't want to explain to Mrs. Parrish why she needed the letter. She needed to find Dethboy's note from the frat computer room and compare it to the one Mrs. Parrish had received. If the two matched, it might help prove that Dethboy was responsible for Peggy's disappearance.

Grabbing her bookbag, Gia left Crane Hall and headed for the library. She wasn't sure they'd let her in after the window-breaking incident Sunday night, but she had to get some work done. She was falling way behind.

As she climbed the stairs, trying to hide her face under her hair, someone in front of her called, "Heads up!"

Gia saw Lee coming down the steps toward her.

"You don't look so great," he said.

Gia grinned. "Thanks a lot."

Lee took Gia's arm and steered her away from the library. "Come on," he said. "I've got to tell you something."

They sat down across from a fountain.

"So, did you find Wally last night?" Gia asked.

Lee shook his head. "He was supposed to be fixing computers, but the tech-head never showed up. No one knows where he is."

Gia frowned.

"I did talk with Peter, though," Lee continued. "I showed him that voice box you found next to Wally's computer."

"And..." Gia prompted.

Lee shrugged. "Peter had no clue. Never saw it before."

Gia thought about her disturbing run-in with Peter at the gym the night before. "And you believed him?" she asked.

"Yeah, I think so. He had no idea what it was. Look," Lee went on. "I was in the library going through last year's newspapers. I was hoping I'd find something about that girl you said disappeared."

Gia nodded. "Yeah, Rebecca. A year ago Friday."

"Every newspaper from last year at this time is gone," Lee told her. "I tried microfiche, and that was missing, too."

Gia groaned inwardly. Dethboy must have gotten to the records! Now she wouldn't be able to prove that this had happened to someone else.

Still...why didn't anyone remember what had happened to Rebecca? Suddenly, Gia had a terrible thought. Maybe Rebecca didn't even exist! Adrian could have made the whole thing up—and stolen the records so no one could disprove it.

"I want to believe you," Lee was saying. "But every time I try to check out your story, I come up empty-handed."

Lee paused, then looked away from her. "Gia, I can't help but think...yesterday morning, when you were caught in the library...did you take last year's papers?"

Gia's jaw dropped open. Lee was doubting her just like she was doubting Adrian! But Lee was supposed to be her friend...Gia looked up into his face and saw concern in his eyes.

Concern...or was it pity? He really does think I'm going crazy, Gia realized.

Just then, a group of sorority sisters passed by. They were taunting a frail-looking girl who walked head down, books clutched tightly in her hands.

"Oh, man," Lee said. "I hate this. Look familiar?"

Gia nodded in stunned silence. When she'd first come to Wintervale, Jenny had singled Gia out as the object of her wrath. There didn't appear to be a reason. Gia had been in the wrong place at the wrong time.

The tormented girl came fully into view. Blond hair, designer clothes…

Jenny.

Gia was shocked. Jenny looked like a wreck. Her hair hadn't been washed. Her makeup had run. She looked like a broken doll.

"What's the matter, Dvorak?" said a red-haired sorority sister. "Hard day?"

The rest of the girls burst out laughing.

When they reached the fountain, the red-haired girl put her arm around Jenny. "I want you to know something. None of us like you. None of us ever liked you. You were nothing when you came to this school. Then the Dvoraks found out you were their kid. We wanted to have parties at their house. We wanted to cruise in limos. Having to put up with you was the price we had to pay. But that's all over now, sweetie. You are out of this sorority!"

The other girls closed in on Jenny, who glared back at them. "Are you finished?" Jenny asked coldly.

A girl dressed all in black sniffed the air and said, "Ooooh, something's ripe out here!"

"Maybe it needs a bath," said the redhead, suddenly shoving Jenny toward the fountain. Jenny stumbled back, dropping her books.

Lee jumped to his feet, but it was too late. The girl in black put her leg out and tripped Jenny. For an instant, Jenny hung in midair. Then she fell backward into the fountain. The sorority sisters collapsed in laughter.

Lee pushed past the girls to the edge of the fountain. Their laughter ceased when they saw the angry look on his face. He pulled Jenny out of the fountain and gently set her down on the grass. Gia followed him over, staring at the sorority sisters.

"What's wrong with you people?" Gia asked. "Don't you have anything better to do?"

"Keep out of it, Gibson," said the redhead. "Unless you want some, too."

Lee gave them a warning look. One by one, the sisters turned and left.

Jenny was crying. Lee held her close.

"What happened?" Gia asked. "Why did they turn on you?"

Jenny looked at Gia strangely, then gave a short laugh. "Yeah, right. Like I'm gonna tell you anything after what happened."

Gia had no idea what Jenny was talking about. Jenny looked away and wiped her face. "I must look like a drowned rat."

"Tell us what happened," Lee said. "Maybe we can help."

Jenny rose unsteadily and started picking up her books. "The Dvoraks," she said. "They lost it all. They trusted this guy to invest for them. And he did. In his own Swiss bank account."

"Someone stole their money?" Gia asked. She wondered why Jenny was referring to her parents by their last name.

"The guy took off last night and fled the country," Jenny said, trembling. "No one knows where he went. He's gone, the money's gone, and everybody hates me..."

"You've still got each other," Lee said. "You never had a family before, Jen. They love you. You're their daughter."

Jenny lowered her head and nodded bitterly. She snatched up the last of her books and said, "It would have been better for them if I'd stayed missing, know what I mean?"

"No, I don't," Lee said.

Jenny shrugged, touching the side of Lee's face. "I'm glad. You're better off."

She smiled sadly at Lee and Gia, then walked away.

Suddenly, a familiar figure came around the fountain. It was Brian Donachy from campus security. He held a large plastic bag in his hands.

"Ms. Gibson!" Donachy called out. "I'm glad I caught up with you."

Before Gia could respond, Donachy pulled a torn black dress from the bag he was holding. "Look familiar?" he asked, dangling it before Gia's face.

"Your party dress," Lee said slowly.

Gia nodded. It was hers all right. But someone had torn it. And part of the dress had been burned.

"You went into my room?" Gia demanded.

"Nope," said Donachy. "I found this in Mark Anderson's room."

Gia shook her head. "I don't even know anyone named Mark Anderson. That's impossible."

"Of course you're going to deny it," Donachy said with a smirk. "But the fact is, your dress was stuffed in the ventilation shaft of Mark's room. Ripped up, just like the clothes you left for that guy." Donachy paused for effect. "The fire started in Mark's room. You started it, Gia. Admit it."

Gia almost laughed out loud. "You're crazy!"

Then she saw the way Lee was staring at her. Her heart sank. He believed Donachy's lies. She could tell. "Lee, please don't listen to anything he says—"

"I'm sorry," Lee said. "But I think you need help. Just leave me alone for a while, all right?"

Lee walked away. Gia started after him. She wanted another chance to explain. And he still had the voice box—her only shred of evidence.

Donachy stopped her. "I'm not finished with you yet. You haven't heard the best part."

Gia waited.

"What I've got on you is circumstantial evidence. Not enough to get you arrested. But it was enough to convince the dean of students that you're a campus menace. Pack your bags and be out of Wintervale by Friday, Ms. Gibson. You're expelled…"

10

Gia stared at her computer screen. It was almost nine at night. She was moments away from her meeting with the Fraternity. She'd been on-line for close to an hour, hoping to catch some glimpse of Lord Myron. But the poet-who-didn't-know-it hadn't appeared in the Rat.

Kindred: Beware of things you do not yet understand!!!
Desdemona: Most gracious hosts, to my unfolding lend a gracious ear: Desire breeds the most desperate form of madness!

Gia switched to another room.

Cloud Dancing: Hello? Anyone like talk to Native American?
Mosi: Cloud Dancing, Ya'at'eeh? Haashyit'eego keehot'i? -Cat
Red Sonia: Bond, I want to thank you for this weekend, darling, I had a wonderful time. I'm sorry for the quick farewell, but you know how it is to be constantly on the run. I'm looking forward to Rio next month. Ciao my darling.
Bond: Red Sonia, As a matter of fact my dear, I just happen to be jetting into

JFK this week on the redeye, any sugges-
tions as to where we should meet, Tavern
on the Green, perhaps…

Gia couldn't help but smile. Bond and Red
Sonia certainly seemed to be getting along.
She checked her watch and realized it was time
to make her appearance.

Taking out last night's printouts from the
Rat, Gia typed in the secret codes the Fraternity had given her. She found herself in a
private room with eight other people.

> **Penndragon:** Greetings, Night Beest.
> **Night Beest:** Greetings.

Gia waited for Penndragon to respond. Then she
realized *they* were waiting for *her*. It was a
test.

Last time, she'd said "yes" to a question in
Japanese. Peter had translated it as "Do you
believe in the Silence?" Now she knew what was
expected of her.

> **Night Beest:** I believe in the Silence.
> **Taliesin:** The Fraternity of Silence is
> listening.

"Cool," Gia whispered.

> **Night Beest:** Where is Dethboy?

Gia held her breath. Yesterday, when she'd

mentioned his name, they'd hurled her from the
Rat.

Merlin: What do you want with the errand
boy?

"Oh, man," Gia murmured, her heart thundering.
There was no question: Dethboy was part of the
Fraternity!

Night Beest: Dethboy lost something that
belonged to him. I know who has it.
Penndragon: Tell us something we don't
know.
Night Beest: It's not Gibson.

Gia waited.

Taliesin: It's Faceless. Challenging us.
Penndragon: Watch what you say.

Gia sat back in her chair. Who in the world
was Faceless?

Merlin: Tell us who has the device. It
has value to us.
Night Beest: Why? There's more than one,
isn't there?

As the silence stretched on, Gia realized
she'd made a mistake.

Penndragon: It's not Faceless.
Taliesin: But it is. Meinichi is at hand.
Romulus and Remus are almost in place.

The targets are ready. I tell you, Faceless is testing us!
Merlin: Enough. Night Beest, who has the
device?

Gia knew that her next words were crucial. She
had to stay in control. She couldn't afford
another mistake.

Night Beest: Not so fast. This is my
game. My rules.
Penndragon: What do you want?

Gia thought fast. They were afraid of Faceless. She'd use it to her advantage.

Night Beest: The coffeehouse. Tomorrow at
noon. All of you. Everyone wears something red. Sit together. I'll be Faceless
no more.
Penndragon: Give us a moment to consider.

Nothing happened for almost a minute. Gia
began to feel a tightness in her stomach. What
was going on?

Suddenly, a small window opened at the top of
her screen. It said IM at the top. Internal
messaging. She'd had no idea the Rat had that
capability. A message that only she could read
flashed into the window.

Goldeneye: Gia, it's a trap! They're
tracing your line, trying to find out who
you are!

Gia stared at her screen with a mixture of amazement and fear. She clicked on the box.

Night Beest: Adrian?
Goldeneye: Meet me at the back door of the old library. Pull the rip cord, Gia. They've almost found you, and I can't throw them off. Do it, now!

Gia yanked her phone line out of the wall. She looked back at her screen. The internal message was frozen there.

Had the IM really come from Adrian? It didn't sound like him. Besides, he was supposed to be mountain climbing with the three guys who'd accused her of stalking them.

Goldeneye must have been monitoring the Fraternity without their knowledge, lurking in a way that was beyond the ability of any programmer she knew. Even Wally. Adrian was supposed to be an acting student, not a computer guru.

Goldeneye had been spying on the Fraternity. And he'd been spying on her.

"So who are you?" Gia whispered. She knew there was only one way to find out. She grabbed her coat and left her room.

Gia made her way toward the outskirts of campus. A couple with a radio passed by.

"Greetings! Val your deejay here, welcoming you to KLRK—late night, every night! So—are you wondering whodunit?"

Gia stopped short, her heart pounding.

"Wonder no more," Val said. "It was Colonel Mustard in the Billiard Room with an ax. And that's ax as in *guitar*! Let's listen to the Colonel's latest…"

Gia hurried on to the old library. As she waited in the woods behind the abandoned building, she thought about what Taliesin had said. He'd mentioned two targets. Romulus and Remus.

Could that mean Rebecca and Peggy?

Suddenly, Gia heard footsteps. She turned and saw Darren moving past her toward the back door of the library. He glanced around suspiciously, his expression cold and lifeless.

Was Darren the one who'd brought her here? She watched him shove open the back door to the library and slip inside. He came out with a parcel wrapped in brown paper and stood under one of the lamp posts. Tearing it open, he revealed a fantastic piece of art.

Darren stared at the painting with awe and excitement. Gia could tell that he was seeing it for the first time. She was confused. She'd

seen his work before, and this looked just
like it.

Gia watched as Darren's expression changed to
resentment. Fascinated, she moved a little
closer. A twig snapped, and Darren spun in her
direction. Her first impulse was to bolt into
the woods, but she was tired of running away.
She stepped into the open.

"You!" Darren screamed, flinging the painting
to the ground. He advanced on Gia, his face
red, his eyes wide and bulging. He looked like
someone out to get her.

Someone like Dethboy.

Gia snatched up a thick branch to defend herself. "Don't come any closer!"

Darren stopped. His chest was heaving. "You're
it, aren't you?" he snarled. "Leonardo. The
Lurker. Whatever you call yourself."

Gia stared at him blankly. "The Lurker?"

Darren hesitated. "No, that doesn't make sense.
You just got to Wintervale. You couldn't be
him. But he told you to make the drop, right?"

"The paintings," Gia said, the truth slowly
dawning on her. "They're not your work."

Darren laughed bitterly. "No kidding."

"Who's the Lurker?"

Darren's shoulders sank. He shook his head and
sat down on the ground. "I think I just said
too much. I'll probably end up like Jenny now.
Or worse."

"What are you talking about?" Gia asked, low-
ering the branch.

"You're gonna turn me in, right? Tell everyone
I'm a fake? Go ahead. I'm not going to try and
stop you."

"Did the Fraternity send you?" Gia asked, more
confused than ever.

Darren frowned. "Zeta Omega?"

"No." Gia swallowed hard. He didn't know what
she was talking about. "Don't you get it? I
liked you. Why do you think I was working so
hard the other night to impress you?"

"The dress, all that—it was for me?"

Gia nodded. "And look how you paid me back.
You believed those lies about me and convinced
Lee that I'm crazy."

He looked away. "Sorry."

"That's it?" Gia demanded. "That's all you
have to say?"

Darren shrugged. Gia wondered how she ever could have wanted to go out with him.

"So what are you going to do?" he asked. "Are you going to tell everyone?"

Gia shook her head. "No. Just *go*. I'm meeting someone."

Darren looked stunned. "You really aren't going to tell anyone, are you?"

"No, I'm not."

"All right. So, what do you want in return?"

"Nothing. What kind of person do you think I am?"

Darren hesitated, as if realizing he'd made a mistake. "Um...all I'm saying is, I've been a jerk, and I want to make it up to you. Isn't there something I can do?"

Gia thought for a moment. Actually, there *was* something she needed. And Darren could help her get it. "The note. I need the note that guy left behind after he hit you in the computer room."

Darren nodded. "Done."

"And the videotape from the party."

"I'll make you a copy. That way, no one'll notice it's missing."

"Perfect."

Darren picked up the painting and started to leave. "Check your mailbox at the student union in the morning. I'll leave the stuff in an envelope for you."

"Thanks," Gia said.

Darren nodded, then walked back toward campus, quickly disappearing from view.

Gia checked her watch. Suddenly, she heard a sound behind her. Before she could turn, an arm wrapped around her body. A hand came down over her mouth. She tried to struggle, but her arms were pinned to her sides.

Helpless, she was dragged back into the dark woods...

11

Gia struggled, but it was no use. Someone was dragging her farther and farther away from the old library. Branches scratched her face as she was dragged deep into the woods.

In the dim moonlight, Gia could see her captor's coat cuff. It was pea green! Then a cold metallic voice spoke to her. A voice she knew all too well.

"I'm not going to hurt you, Gia," Dethboy said. "I'm not who you think I am."

Gia squirmed in Dethboy's arms. She tried to shout for help, but Dethboy's gloved hand was clamped firmly over her mouth. He held her so tight, the self-defense skills Wally had taught her were useless.

"Stop fighting me and listen. Tomorrow, you'll be told that Adrian wandered away from the climb and was lost in the mountains. Don't believe it. Nothing is as it seems, Gia. It wasn't Adrian talking to you on-line earlier today, but you already suspected that. Trust Goldeneye. Your life, and the lives of your friends, may depend on it."

The gloved hand abruptly came away from Gia's mouth. "Lee?"

"I don't think so." Dethboy laughed as he pressed a cloth soaked in foul-smelling chemicals against Gia's face.

And darkness closed in.

* * *

Someone was shaking her. Gia opened her eyes and saw two girls kneeling beside her.

It was daylight. She was still in the woods. One of the girls was dressed in a leather biker jacket. The other wore a medieval gown. A motorcycle stood nearby.

"Are you okay?" the biker girl asked.

Gia rubbed her head. "Yeah," she said groggily.

"My name's Calle Ann," said the biker girl. "This is Amy. I was just giving her a lift back from a tournament. Good thing we took a shortcut through the woods. Are you sure you're okay?"

Gia nodded as they helped her to her feet.

"You ought to think about going to the infirmary," Amy said.

"I'll be all right," said Gia. "You guys go ahead."

"Okay," Calle Ann said, nodding her head. She and Amy got on the motorcycle. "See ya!"

Gia walked back to campus. She was starved. She got a candy bar from a snack machine in the student union, then checked her mailbox. The package that Darren had promised her last night was there. Gia glanced around quickly and tore it open. Inside, she found the note from Dethboy and the videotape. She also found a letter from Darren.

Gia—

We're even now. I'm sick of owing people.

—D

Suddenly, a group of students came rushing down the stairs. Gia darted out of the way and ran right into Mr. Jordan, her faculty adviser. He looked worried.

"What's going on?" Gia asked him.

Mr. Jordan frowned. "A bunch of students went out climbing yesterday. Last night, one of them wandered off and got lost."

Gia felt a sudden chill. "What's his name?"

"Adrian Straus," Mr. Jordan replied. "Why? Do you know him?"

Stunned, Gia didn't know what to say. "Not really," she finally managed.

Gia left the student union in a haze. She didn't even realize at first that someone was walking next to her, trying to get her attention. When she finally noticed Peter at her side, she stopped dead.

That night in the gym, he'd looked different. Then he'd seemed sinister. Now he just looked confused and upset.

"Did Wally talk to you?" Peter asked.

"What?" Gia asked, trying to focus.

He jammed a piece of paper into Gia's hand. It was an e-mail to Peter from Wally.

To: Ronin
From: Beaker

You know what they say, buddy. When the going gets tough, the wimps like me cut out. I'm not going to stick around for Wally World II. Everyone at Wintervale thinks I'm a joke. So I'm leaving. Hitching to a friend's place in San Francisco. I'll give you a call when I get there. It's been real, and been fun, but...

Gia couldn't believe it. She knew Wally hadn't been seen since Monday—

Then it came to her.

She looked at Peter, doing her best to act normal. "He didn't tell me a thing."

Peter took the note back and shook his head. "I just hope he's okay. Let me know if you hear from him."

"Sure," Gia said as Peter hurried off.

Slowly, Gia turned and started back to Crane Hall. It was all starting to make sense now. Peg had met Troy and taken off with him on Sunday. Wally had left school on Monday. Adrian had gotten lost on Tuesday. It couldn't be coincidence. All of them had been "collected" by the Fraternity.

One for every day this week.

If Gia was right, someone would disappear today. And again, tomorrow. And in both cases there would be a totally believable excuse.

Then Friday. Meinichi. Death Day. Gia shuddered. The day she would disappear.

No. Not if she had anything to say about it. Not only was she here to stay, but by Friday, she'd have Peg back. Safe and sound.

The worst part was that she couldn't tell anyone. The Fraternity—led by Faceless, Leonardo, the Lurker, or whatever this person called himself—had destroyed Gia's credibility. No one would believe her. And if she tried to run, they would just catch her wherever she went.

Gia remembered something Jenny had told her. *You can't win. It's impossible. He doesn't leave Wintervale. If you go, you'll be safe. I wish I had.*

Those words, and what Darren had said last night about someone making him do things, haunted her now.

Gia checked her watch. It was almost noon. No time to go back to Crane Hall to shower and change. The Fraternity was waiting.

Gia hurried to Scribes and Jibes, the campus coffeehouse. It got its name from the poets and comedians who performed there every Friday night.

When she arrived, she looked through the coffeehouse's front window. It was packed inside. Perfect. It would be easy for her to spot eight people sitting together, all wearing something red. But they'd never notice her. She'd be hidden by the crowd.

Taking a deep breath, Gia went inside. At first, she thought she was seeing things. The color red was everywhere. Red sweatshirts. Red jackets. Red scarves. Red gloves. Red hair.

Every single person in the coffeehouse except
her was wearing something red.

A student looked her up and down. "Don't need
a free lunch, huh?"

Gia stared at the blond girl before her.
"Excuse me?"

"Val announced it last night on KLRK. Free
lunch at S'n'J's today for anyone wearing
something red. You missed out."

The girl wandered off into the crowd. Gia's
heart sank. There was no way she could spot
the Fraternity now. They must have gotten Val
to help them. Once again they were invisible—
and yet she was certain they were here. Looking for Night Beest.

That's right, she thought. Looking for someone
standing around gawking. Kinda like you.

Gia turned and was about to leave when she
noticed a woman grinning at her. She came
over, took Gia's arm, and led her to a table.

"Hey, glad you could make it!" the woman said
loudly as they sat down. "Thanks for coming
down to talk to me. I hear you've got some
great new ideas for the show!"

The show? Gia wondered. Then she realized who
the woman was. It had to be Val, the KLRK deejay.

"Pretend you know me," Val said under her breath. "They're watching."

"Forget this," Gia said, starting to get up.

Val grabbed Gia's arm and guided her back into her chair. "I know what you must be thinking. That I'm one of them. Part of the Fraternity."

Gia stared at Val, waiting.

Val smiled. "Well, I'm not. I'm with Golden-eye, and he's trying to help you. He sent the guy in the Dethboy costume last night to warn you. But he *didn't* send the real Dethboy. And he was lurking in the chat room when you met with the Fraternity—he told me about your meeting here with them and sent me to inter-cept you."

"But if that's true, why'd you help the Fra-ternity by telling everyone to wear red?" Gia asked.

"I didn't have a choice. I was taking phone-ins on the air. Some guy called in with this idea about free lunch at S'n'J's today for anyone wearing red. Then three or four more guys called in. Pretty soon, the manager him-self called to say, 'Let's do it!' What was I supposed to do? I was stuck. I'm sorry. Believe me, we want to know who these guys are, too."

Val sounded like she was talking about warring

families. Suddenly Gia remembered what Dethboy had said while he was chasing her across campus: "We're like Romeo and Juliet." The Capulets and the Montagues. *Warring families.* Dethboy had been hinting at something like that, but could Gia believe any of it? Gia got up. She needed time to think. "I gotta get something to eat. I'll be back."

Over at the counter, she took a plate and wondered if she had enough money for lunch. Someone jostled her. She looked up and immediately recognized the long-haired guy from the dorm. The one who knew her name and had tried to stop her from going upstairs to Wally's room during the fire.

"Sorry about this, Gia," he said quietly. "Nothing personal."

Suddenly, he slammed his tray on the floor. "Why won't you just leave me alone!" he screamed. Everyone fell silent and turned to look at them.

"It's not enough that you torch my room," he went on, "but you plant your dress there, too. Now my girlfriend thinks I'm cheating on her. Just get it through your thick skull, okay? I'm not interested in you. I don't want to date you. I don't want to know you exist!"

With that, he stormed out of the coffeehouse. Gia started to go after him, but Val stepped in front of her.

"Hold on, don't you understand the game they're playing?" Val asked, grabbing Gia's arm. "They *want* you to follow him. That's why you're going to sit right here. I'll follow him and let you know what I find out." Val smiled. "I'll have to make a scene, too. To throw them off. Nothing personal."

Nothing personal, Gia thought. The exact same thing that the long-haired guy had said. Well, *this* would be nothing personal either.

"I've had enough of this," Gia said, raising her voice. "There's no way I'm going to do what you or anybody else tells me to do. You people want me out of here? Fine. I'm expelled, why should I hang around? I'm on the four-thirty bus. Good-bye, Wintervale. Good-bye to *all* of you!"

Val looked around nervously. One person started clapping. Then another. Soon, everyone in the coffeehouse was applauding. Gia yanked her arm away from Val and walked out.

As Gia made her way back to Crane Hall, she considered the move she'd just made. She was pretty sure the Fraternity had planned to take her on Friday. Now she was forcing them to make their move today.

Her plan was risky, and she knew it. But somehow she had to take control.

When she got back to the dorm, Gia found a

note stuck to her door from an overnight delivery service. The package from Peggy's parents had arrived. Marissa had signed for it.

Gia went down the hall to Marissa's room. Three other students were already camped out there. The door was closed. "Is Marissa busy?" Gia asked them.

One of the students shook her head. "She's not here. Didn't show up for class this morning, either. And she didn't let anyone know she was taking off. Weird, huh?"

Gia nodded. "I guess I'll come back," she said.

Walking back to her room, Gia thought about the disappearing students, one each day. Peggy on Sunday. Wally on Monday. Adrian on Tuesday. And today?

Gia looked back at the three students standing outside Marissa's door and knew she had her answer...

12

Gia sat in the bleachers, waiting for football practice to break up. She waved to Lee as he headed off the field, and he jogged over to join her. Before he could say anything, Gia held out a bus ticket.

"You're going home," Lee said, surprised.

"No," Gia said. "I'm not."

Lee looked at her in confusion.

"They're planning on taking me," Gia explained. "Just like they took Peg, Wally, and Adrian. They wanted to do it Friday, but now they have to do it today, before I get on the bus. I need you to be there when they try to grab me."

Lee looked away from her. "I just don't buy it, G. I'm sorry. Peggy met some guy and ran off with him. Wally had a meltdown—everyone could see that coming. This guy Adrian got lost on a climb. I don't see a conspiracy."

"Of course you don't. That's the whole point." Gia sighed, frustrated. "All right. What about the voice box I gave you?"

"I'll get it," he said. He looked at her ticket. "I'll bring it to the bus stop."

"Fine," Gia said, giving up. "I guess I'll see you there."

She got up and strode away from Lee. As she made her way back to Crane Hall, she chose a well-populated route. The Fraternity would have a hard time getting to her in broad daylight with lots of students around.

Gia had been counting on Lee's support. Now she was on her own. When she reached her dorm room, she locked the door and propped a chair up against it. Then she sat down in front of her computer and checked her mail. A note was waiting from Goldeneye, telling her where to meet him. She quickly got on the campus net and found him.

> **Goldeneye:** I hear you're leaving.
> **Night Beest:** Word travels fast. Especially when you have the Fraternity filling you in.
> **Goldeneye:** Gia, you have to trust me.
> **Night Beest:** I don't have to do anything. I'm not like Darren and Jenny and Val and that long-haired guy.
> **Goldeneye:** Mark Anderson. The fire started in his room.
> **Night Beest:** I know that. I know a lot more than you think I do. You wanted me to see Darren pick up that painting. To

see if I'd use him the way you use him.
But I didn't fall for it. And what about
Jenny? What happened to her was because
of me, right? She warned me to go and
that would have messed up your plans. So
you got even with her.

Goldeneye didn't respond.

Night Beest: I heard that Jenny didn't
have anything when she got to Wintervale.
Then all of sudden she's rich. She cross-
es you and all that goes away. Then
there's Darren. He doesn't do his own
paintings. If it got out that he's a
fake, he'd be ruined. That's how you control people. And now you want me. I don't
know why, but you do.
Goldeneye: I want to help you. We have
common enemies.
Night Beest: Yeah, right. You want me to
believe that it's you and your people
against the Fraternity.
Goldeneye: That's right.
Night Beest: I don't think so. I think
you had someone take Peg and the others.
I think everyone's working for you. If I
found Peg and the others with your help,
I would have owed you. And I would have
been trapped, just like Jenny and Darren.
Goldeneye: Listen to me. There is another
threat. Someone who was close to me once,
but no longer.
Night Beest: You've been lying to me from
the beginning. You make up names. Leonar-

do, Lurker, Faceless. You make people think you're their best friend. Then you nail them. Well, I don't know who you are, and I don't care. But I'm not playing the game anymore.

Gia yanked the phone line out of the wall, then turned off her computer. For the first time in a long time, she felt in control.

*   *   *

All day, Gia made sure to stay in public places. The new library. The student union. The quad. No one bothered her. She told herself that all she had to do was get on that bus. When the Lurker saw she was gone, he would release Peg and the others. It was that simple.

But she knew in her heart that nothing was ever that simple...

"*Warriors unite!*" several guys on the quad cheered. Gia noticed dozens of students heading toward the football field.

"What's up?" Gia asked one of them.

"Pep rally," the guy said. "You coming?"

Gia nodded and fell in with the crowd. It occurred to her that Lee wouldn't have been able to help her even if he'd wanted to. He had to be at the rally.

She found a seat in the top row of the bleachers. People surrounded her on all sides. There
was no way for anyone to get near her unde-
tected. The rally picked up swiftly. Soon the
Wintervale Warriors were racing onto the
field. Gia watched as number 42 ran out to the
cheers of the crowd.

"Go get 'em, Lee," Gia said sadly.

Students wearing green-and-yellow capes and
Roman-style helmets circulated through the
crowd. They were the "squires"—students who
helped drum up enthusiasm in the stands.

On the field, Coach Aziz took the microphone
and the crowd went wild. Everyone rose to
their feet, applauding and cheering. The band
played "We Are the Champions" and the crowd
started singing along.

Gia couldn't help herself. She began to sing
with them. Just then, someone grabbed her arm.
She realized there was a squire on either side
of her. One of them held her firmly as the
other lifted a familiar-smelling piece of
cloth toward her face.

It was happening. The Fraternity had come for
her!

This time, Gia was prepared. She ducked away
from the cloth and thrust herself toward the
squire holding her arm. Hitting him squarely
with her shoulder, she knocked him off bal-

ance. He toppled backward, dragging down other students as he fell.

The other squire tried to grab her from behind, but Gia brought her heel down hard on his instep. He howled in pain. Gia grabbed the smelly cloth from his hand and reached for his helmet. Before she could hit him with the chloroform-soaked rag, he and the other squire darted away through the crowd.

Gia wanted to race after them, but she noticed something lying on the bleacher. One of the squires had dropped a small black computer disk. And another student was about to step on it.

Suddenly, a bulky figure wearing sunglasses and a bandanna grabbed the student and pushed him to the side. Gia reached down and picked up the disk. Then she recognized the guy in the sunglasses. It was Lee! Glancing at the playing field, she saw number 42 still out there, his helmet obscuring his face.

Lee held his hand out to Gia. Together, they left the bleachers and made their way across campus.

"What's going on?" Gia asked.

"I got someone to take my place in the rally. I was worried about you. You're right. A lot of what's been going on doesn't add up."

Gia closed her eyes and leaned up against Lee. He was finally coming around. "Did you see them?" Gia asked. "Those squires tried to grab me!"

Lee nodded. "Yeah. You did good back there."

Gia smiled. She held up the rag. "Take a whiff of this. Not too much. You'll end up passing out."

Lee shook his head. "No thanks. I can smell it from here."

Gia noticed an old plastic bag on the grass. She picked it up and stuck the smelly rag inside. "That's called evidence, counselor."

Lee nodded. "Let's head back to your room and see what's on that disk."

Back at Crane Hall, Gia loaded the disk and checked its directory. About a dozen files were there, some starting with Deth, others with Gia, Wally, Peg, and Adrian. Gia ran one of the Deth files.

Suddenly, her computer screen was filled with garish colors and bizarre images. "This is what it looked like when I was being dragged to Dethboy's lair!" Gia exclaimed.

As if on cue, Dethboy's lair appeared. Gia opened a bunch of files. In one she found the Oath of the Fraternity of Silence.

Lee read it aloud. "'To prove yourself to me,
you must be willing to do what others are not.
The lives of lesser beings are unimportant to
the Lurker or to his Fraternity...'"

Lee shook his head as Gia scanned through
multiple screens. "It's all here," he said.
"Everything you told me. Those guys must
really be paranoid to keep a disk like this
on them."

Gia nodded. She opened another file, and a
list of names appeared. She recognized two
of them right away: Ted Leonetti and Mark
Anderson. She clicked on Leonetti's name and
a file opened up called "The Lurker's Student
Bodies—Ted Leonetti."

Gia read about how the Lurker had trapped
Leonetti. Ted's father had been embezzling
from his company for years. Ted either did
what the Lurker said or his father's crime
would be revealed. The file revealed that
Ted had been forced to lodge a false complaint against Gia, and that the disappearances were part of the Fraternity's initiation
ceremonies.

Gia sat back. "They're taking people to prove
themselves to the Lurker. He's here on campus
somewhere. If the cops could find him, they'd
find Peg and the others!"

"You might be right," Lee said. He reached past
Gia and popped the disk out of her computer.

"Come on," Gia said. "Let's take that to the police."

"Sorry, G," Lee said, his expression cold. "We're not going anywhere."

Lee smacked the computer disk against her desk. Once, twice, three times, until it cracked in half.

Gia stared at him, realizing the awful mistake she'd made.

Lee worked for the Lurker…

13

Gia stared at Lee in stunned silence. Keeping his gaze fixed on Gia, he picked up the bag containing the chloroform-soaked cloth. He dropped the cracked disk into the bag.

"See ya soon, G.," Lee said, leaving the room.

Gia sat back and exhaled slowly. Lee was part of the Lurker's Fraternity! But why hadn't he tried to take her? Then it hit her: The Fraternity was sticking with their plan. They'd collect her on Friday. There was no way out, and no one she could trust.

Gia went to the door and locked it. They wanted her to be afraid.

Too bad.

She returned to her computer. The Dethboy program was still on screen. She printed out what was there—the evidence about Ted Leonetti.

Gia thought of the account she'd read of Peg's murder. That was the first thing she'd seen in Dethboy's lair, but she'd hardly given it any thought. The account had been brutal and ugly. Not something she'd wanted to dwell on. But...

Come on, Gia, she told herself. You want to be a journalist, think like one.

She considered everything that had happened Sunday night. Everything she'd seen, everything she'd been told. She remembered Dethboy's first words to her:

"I see you, Gia…YOU'RE NEXT."

Gia had assumed that he meant, "I know you're in my lair, I know who you are." But could there be another meaning? An idea came to her. It was so crazy, and yet…Gia wondered if he actually was seeing her. It would explain so much.

She glanced at the window. The curtains were drawn. No one could see in. She looked around the room. Maybe there was a hole in the wall that someone could see through. She tried not to be obvious about what she was doing, just in case…

Nothing. But there was one last possibility. Gia went to her bed and collapsed as if she were exhausted. Scanning the ceiling through half-closed eyes, she found what she was looking for. In the corner was a spider's web. And behind that web, something small and round looked out at her, like a cold, alien eye.

A camera. Aimed directly at her computer screen.

Gia casually shifted her gaze away. Her heart was pounding. What was it Dana Scully had said in the Rat?

Just because I'm paranoid doesn't mean they're not out to get me.

The Fraternity was watching her every move, on-line and off. They must have known that she was Night Beest all along! Gia felt an icy determination rising within her. Dethboy had given her one clue about what was really going on. There could be other clues in the things he'd said and done. And *written*.

She needed help, and she knew where to get it. But she'd need a computer. She couldn't use hers anymore. She picked up some of her books, sliding the package with the videotape between them, and left her room.

In the hallway, she scanned for other cameras. She saw none. A couple of girls walked by. Gia waited until they were in their rooms, then sneaked upstairs. She slipped past the barricades that had been put up by the fire marshal at the second-floor landing.

The smell of smoke was overpowering. She could see why the second floor was still off-limits. The overhead lights were on in parts of the hallway—there was still electricity, despite the fire damage.

Gia tried every door until she found one that

had been left unlocked. She slipped inside.
There was no VCR to play her tape, but there
was a computer. Gia powered it up. She used a
screen name she had seen before, TwiliZone,
then logged on to the Mystery Forum of the
campus net.

TwiliZone: I've got a mystery none of you
people can solve.
Bond: I'm sure we can rise to the challenge.
TwiliZone: Someone just borrowed three
students from Wintervale and is hiding
them somewhere on campus. I'll give you
some clues. Tell me where to find the
missing students.
Red Sonia: And I thought this was going
to be hard.
Lethe's Dream: Play on, brave TwiliZone.

Gia typed in an account of what had happened
to her since she'd been drawn into Dethboy's
lair. She changed the names and details that
might give her away. Dethboy became Corpseface, Peg became Meg, and so on. She finished,
then waited for a response.

Spectre: We like the camera in the room.
Creepy.

A campus map appeared in a window on Gia's
screen. Someone must have pulled it up for all
to see.

Red Sonia: They'd have to hold the people

in a building no one ever goes to. How
about one of the new buildings under con-
struction?
Bond: More likely it would be one that
was abandoned or not in use.
Griff: TwiliZone, are you sure the missing students are still on campus?

Gia wasn't one hundred percent sure of anything right now. But it made sense to her.

TwiliZone: Yes. There are clues in the
description of the roommate's murder.
It's set in an old burned-out place. But
I can't think of anywhere on campus that
burned down and wasn't rebuilt.
Spectre: Wait a minute. The confession
you typed in only "implied" a burned-out
building. It could just be old and in
ruins.
Lethe's Dream: Hey, Corpseface was quot-
ing Byron. Maybe Lord Myron's behind it
all!
Draco: Too obvious. Corpse also mentions
Romeo and Juliet. And this secret society
likes to talk in Japanese terms like
meinichi.
Bond: I agree. We seem to be dealing with
a literary crowd.
TwiliZone: Draco, what did you mean about
meinichi?
Spectre: I can answer that. We learned
about this in sociology. The literal
translation of meinichi is Death Day, but
it's not meant to be sinister. Just the

opposite. Meinichi is a day when families gather to remember the people they've lost. It's said that on meinichi, the dead come back to walk among the living. It's like a family reunion. A party.

Gia felt a sudden chill. In Dethboy's lair, Peg's photo had been changed to make it look as if she'd been murdered. And when she'd heard Peg's voice on the phone, she'd said they'd be together Friday, for some kind of party.

Could Peg be behind all this? But she and Peg had always gotten along! On the other hand, both Val and Mark had told her that this was nothing personal. Maybe that was another clue.

TwiliZone: Come on, guys. Where are the missing people?
Red Sonia: It would have to be a building on the outer edge of campus, where people could easily go in and out without being seen.
Bond: Good show, mon amour…
Red Sonia: You flatter me, darling.
Draco: I still think those literary references are clues.

Gia stared at the campus map. Romeo and Juliet. Byron. A Japanese/English dictionary…

"Books," Gia whispered excitedly.

TwiliZone: The old library! You guys got
it! Good work!
Red Sonia: Ciao!

Gia logged off and shut down the computer. She
picked up her books and the videotape and left
the room. A sound came from the stairs. Before
she could find a place to take cover, someone
appeared on the landing.

Marissa.

Gia stared at the R.A. in amazement. She'd
been certain that Marissa had been chosen by
the Fraternity for Wednesday. If she was
wrong, then who would they take today?

"Gia, what are you doing?" Marissa called out.
"Second floor's off-limits."

Gia thought fast. "I heard someone up here, so
I came up to check it out. But I couldn't find
anyone. Hey, do you have that package for me?
The one from Mrs. Parrish?"

Gia started down the stairs with Marissa.
"Someone broke into my room while I was out
today," Marissa explained. "A whole bunch of
stuff got taken, including your delivery. I'm
sorry."

Gia nodded. Somehow, this didn't really surprise her. The Fraternity had broken into her
own room to plant the camera and to steal her

dress to use as evidence for Donachy.

Marissa stopped before her door and shoved it open. It wobbled a little. The doorknob looked as if someone had beaten it with a hammer.

Gia looked inside. She had to hide her excitement. "It's a miracle they didn't take the TV and VCR."

"I guess it would have been too hard to conceal or whatever," Marissa said. "Could you do me a favor? Wait here until I get back with campus security?"

"Sure," said Gia.

Marissa headed off down the hall. Gia slipped into the room and closed the door behind her. She looked around for cameras, but didn't see any. She loaded the videotape Darren had given her into the VCR and turned it on, along with the TV.

The tape showed the party from Sunday night. Gia hoped it would contain clues about Dethboy's identity. Dethboy had struck Darren in the dark, left a note, then fled the computer room. There was no way he would've worn his costume to the party. He would have wanted to blend in with the other students. If the tape showed the lights coming back on and someone running into the party from the computer room, Gia would have a prime suspect for Dethboy.

The tape began to play. Gia watched as she and Lee came through the front door. The cameraman was moving around the room. He focused in on Darren and a few of his friends.

"You're gonna ask Gonzo Gibson out?" one of the guys asked. "She's a psycho!"

Darren didn't look happy. "She's all right," he insisted. "Those guys made everything up because she wouldn't go out with any of them."

Gia froze the tape on a close-up of Darren. Could the Lurker have ordered him to talk to her at the party? Darren did seem awfully uncomfortable defending her to his friends. And she knew that he owed the Lurker. So nothing he said or did could be trusted.

Gia thought back to the night of the party. Darren had taken her into the Rat and promised to get her onto the student newspaper. If it had worked, she would have owed him. No, not Darren—she would have owed the Lurker.

The Lurker had tried to make her believe that his operatives were pitted against a group called the Fraternity. But Gia didn't buy it. As far as she was concerned, the Lurker had set up this game to trap her into becoming one of his operatives.

But something didn't make sense. If she was right, and *everyone* was working for the Lurker, why had Dethboy interrupted her and Darren in the computer room? If Dethboy and Darren were on the same side, wouldn't Dethboy have left Darren alone to bring her under the Lurker's influence?

Could the Lurker have been telling the truth? It would explain why Lee hadn't tried to capture her when he had the chance. The *Fraternity* wanted Gia taken, not the Lurker. It would also explain why Lee had destroyed the disk the Fraternity guy had dropped. The disk had contained evidence that the Lurker was responsible for the disappearances. It had convinced her that the Lurker was behind it all.

But now it was starting to look like the Fraternity really was a separate group. A group of people trying to bring down the Lurker.

So maybe Faceless, the leader of the Fraternity, and the Lurker, the figure controlling Lee, Jenny, and Darren, weren't the same, as she had believed. And, for some reason, she was caught in the middle.

"No," she whispered. "Not for some reason. For a specific reason."

But what was it?

Gia scanned forward on the tape. She saw Wally enter the party. He looked around nervously, then disappeared into the crowd. The power went off soon after. Darkness. Confusion. When the lights came back on, Wally was hurrying toward a long-haired guy Gia knew all too well: Mark Anderson. Gia was certain he was part of the Fraternity from the way he'd acted at the coffeehouse today.

There was something on Wally's shirt. Not punch. Blood. Gia couldn't tell whether Wally had come from the computer room, but he was acting nervous and upset.

Wally and Mark talked, both of them glancing anxiously back toward the computer room. They left the party within seconds of each other. Then Darren and Gia came into the room.

Gia scanned the tape back and froze it on the image of Wally and Mark leaving the party together. Was one of them leaving to go put on the Dethboy costume and lie in wait for her?

Gia touched the screen image of Wally. She'd thought he was her friend. "Not you, too."

But she couldn't deny it any longer. Wally *was* in the Fraternity.

14

The sun was beginning to set when Gia reached the old library. She was surprised to find no sentries posted outside. Of course, they wouldn't look like guards. They would appear to be a couple of students hanging out. The Fraternity's strength was in being able to operate in plain view.

Gia decided not to go in the back door. She found an open window on the side of the building and slipped through.

The library seemed completely deserted. Empty bookcases, overturned chairs, and broken tables filled the room. The Lurker had sent her here before, which lent credibility to her theory that the Lurker was behind all her troubles. Still…

Suddenly, Gia heard a sound. A door opening. Footsteps coming her way. She looked around, saw a small room nearby, and darted into it. The room was empty, except for a small desk. There were no doors or windows in the room.

The footsteps were coming closer. Had someone seen her?

Gia scanned the room, looking for a way out.

Then she saw it. An air-conditioning vent. She climbed up on the desk and tugged at the metal grill. It came loose on one side and swung down. She hauled herself into the vent and was about to replace the grill when someone entered the room. She scrambled deeper into the narrow shaft.

"Come on, Ted," said a familiar voice. It was Mark Anderson. "Don't get weird on me, man. It was probably just a squirrel or something that got in when we weren't watching."

"Okay, okay," said another guy. "We'd better get back outside."

The footsteps receded. Mark had called his companion Ted. It must have been that Leonetti guy who'd filed complaints against her.

Gia heard other voices echoing down the shaft. She crawled toward them, passing vents that opened onto other darkened rooms. Finally, she came to a lit room. She stopped near the opening and peered down.

In the room below she saw him. It was Wally. He was pacing back and forth in front of a computer. He spoke into a small microphone, and a distorted, electronic voice answered him. Though she couldn't read what was on the screen, Gia could see lines of text appearing whenever one of them spoke.

"We need to pull out," Wally was saying.

"The Boy Scout got ahold of the evidence we planted. And the fact that he didn't just haul Gia off after he wrecked the disk showed her that this really is *us* against *them*. That the Lurker hasn't been setting her up. I'm sorry, Romulus isn't going to fall. Not this way. We got too elaborate. Next time—"

The electronic voice crackled, cutting Wally off. "We need damage control. That's all."

"We're past damage control!" Wally shouted. "This whole Romulus and Remus thing has gone too far. I know why you did it. I don't blame you. If the Lurker had done to me what he did to you, I'd want to get even, too. But you've been telling me from the start to think about the big picture. What the Lurker's doing is wrong, and we have to stop him. Right?"

"That's right," the voice said.

"Then don't let your personal vendetta get in the way," Wally urged. "Look, none of this has been easy. Could you just come over here so we can talk face-to-face? It's one thing for you to be Faceless to them. You don't have to hide anything with me. You know that."

Faceless didn't reply.

Gia was stunned. Faceless and the Lurker were *not* the same person. There really was some kind of war going on between the Fraternity and the Lurker's operatives.

"We've lost Gia," said Wally. "She could be anywhere. Even off campus by now. Maybe she's already gone to the authorities and made them believe her story—"

"That won't work," said Faceless. "No one will believe her story without proof, and she no longer has it. We have to find another way to give her the evidence."

Wally was quiet for a moment. "We should at least move our guests off campus. I know you picked this place because the Lurker uses it sometimes and you like playing games with him. But we agreed that once Gia went to the police, we would move out. We can't get caught here when they start searching the university."

"Wally, calm down. It's under control."

"No, it isn't. We're supposed to bring in the authorities to uncover the Lurker. Not risk discovery ourselves. We shouldn't be here. I don't understand why we couldn't have just set up off campus to start with."

"The Lurker never leaves here."

"We have to be smarter than the Lurker. Remus has to be better than Romulus."

Only silence came from the computer.

In the airshaft, Gia's heart raced. Who was Faceless? Earlier, Gia thought Faceless might

have been Peg because of the meinichi connection. And Wally always used to ask about Peg
whenever they were on-line. Gia thought it was
just because he had a crush on her. But what
if it was something more? What if Peg was
Faceless? As hard as it was for Gia to accept,
it made sense.

"I'm gonna go check on our special guest,"
Wally said angrily. "Just think about what I
said, all right? Maybe we should consider
using the backup plan instead. Gia's my
friend. I've hated using her like this."

Faceless didn't respond. Wally left the room.

Who was the special guest? Gia wondered.
Adrian, probably. And what did Wally mean by
the backup plan? Then it came to her: Maybe
the Fraternity had been setting up someone
else to take the "evidence" to the authorities, just in case the plan with Gia failed.

Gia shoved at the grill until it came loose.
She carefully climbed down from the vent and
made her way toward the computer. The person
who'd set her up from the beginning was sitting at another terminal, probably somewhere
else on campus, waiting for Wally to return.

Gia considered bringing the authorities to
the old library to free Adrian, but Faceless
wasn't here and would be able to escape.

She cleared her throat and picked up the

microphone, hoping that her voice would sound
as garbled to Faceless as Faceless's voice had
to them. There was something she wanted to
know...

"Faceless, I'm back," Gia said. "I've been
thinking. We should give up on Gia. She was a
bad choice right from the beginning."

The electronic voice crackled. "We've had this
discussion before."

Gia stood her ground. "We're having it again."

There was a brief silence. "We chose Gia Gibson for a reason," Faceless said. "That reason
is still valid. She doesn't suspect you. She
thinks you're her friend. In the beginning,
that made it easy for us to manipulate her.
You knew exactly what you were doing when you
created the Dethboy lair and Wally World."

Gia froze. So Wally *had* done all that.

"But more importantly, her ties to the other
side are still strong. She's friends with Lee.
She has a history with Darren and Jenny. We
knew from the start that whatever we did would
go right back to the Lurker through her. And I
want the Lurker to know what it feels like to
be trapped." Faceless hesitated. "We won't go
to the backup unless Gibson manages to get off
campus."

Gia felt herself losing control. She couldn't

believe people she'd considered friends had
used her like this. Wally. Lee. Peg…

"Wrong," she shouted into the microphone. "You
get over here and you talk to me face-to-face,
or I'm telling everyone that you called the
operation off."

"What?" Faceless asked. "You can't—"

Gia tossed the microphone aside and turned off
the computer. "Sure I can."

She was about to crawl back up into the airshaft when the door swung open and Wally
walked in.

She couldn't believe it. He was wearing a pea
green coat and carrying a Dethboy mask and
voice-altering device!

"Great!" Wally called to the microphone. "Now
they can't even find Darren. I—"

He stopped dead when he spotted Gia. His
shoulders tightened as he looked at her coldly.
Then he saw that the computer had been turned
off, his link to Faceless severed. He rushed
past Gia and turned the machine back on.

"What did you do?" Wally asked, trying to
reestablish the connection with Faceless.

Gia didn't answer. This was it. Wally would
call for help, and the Fraternity would take
her captive. She had to act now.

She was on him, using moves he had taught her.
And he had taught her well. Too well. Wally
had taught her that even a master at Cuong-Nhu
could be taken if his opponent had the element
of surprise. And she *had* surprised him. A
moment later, Wally fell to the floor, uncon-
scious.

Gia couldn't call the authorities. They'd
think she was crazy. She had to find someone
to back up her story. The special guest—it
could very well be Adrian. He was the last one
to go missing.

If she could find Adrian, or someone, to cor-
roborate her story, she wouldn't have to find
files outlining the Fraternity's plans, or
videotapes made from the hidden camera placed
in her room.

Gia noticed an unplugged telephone sitting on
the edge of the computer desk. She plugged the
phone line from the computer into the phone
and dialed a number she had seen in the student newspaper that afternoon.

"KLRK. Val speaking."

"Are we on the air?" Gia asked.

"Nope."

"Good. Do you know who this is?"

"Yes, Gia."

"Well, there's a big party going on right now at the old library. You and your friends wouldn't want to miss it."

Gia hung up, then dialed 911. She was banking on the fact that she would find the special guest before the police arrived.

Gia looked down at Wally. It's my turn to be Dethboy, she thought, as she took the coat off Wally, slipped it on, and pulled the mask over her face. She fitted the voice box into place then went through the coat pockets and found Wally's keys.

Unplugging the phone again, she used the cord to tie Wally's hands behind his back. She found some masking tape in the computer desk and gently placed it over his mouth before leaving the room. She searched the corridors, passing two men who looked vaguely familiar. She nodded at them. They nodded back. The costume did its job.

After they were gone, Gia tried one door after another and found only dark, empty rooms. She turned the corner and tried yet another door.

This one was locked. She took out her keys. She didn't have much time. The third key she tried opened the door. She heard someone inside give a startled gasp as light from the hallway flooded the dark room.

Sitting on the edge of a small cot was her

roommate, Peggy Parrish. Peg was terrified. "I've never seen your face," she whispered. "Please, please let me out of here. I won't tell anyone, I swear!"

Gia was stunned. She'd been all but certain that Peggy was Faceless. But now it was clear that Peg was the backup. She'd been kept isolated, seeing only Dethboy all this time.

But if Peg wasn't Faceless, then who was?

Gia realized she didn't have time to worry about that. Faceless would arrive soon. She put a finger to her mouth, then raised the Dethboy mask to reveal her face. Peg stared at her in confusion.

"I'm here to get you out," Gia said. Peg recoiled from the eerie voice coming from the device Gia wore. Gia realized that she was scaring Peg, but she didn't have time to take it off. They had to get moving. "I'm not one of them. Do you believe me?"

"Them?" Peg asked. She gasped, her gaze suddenly shifting to the door.

Gia slipped the mask back down and spun to face two guys who stood in the doorway, silhouetted by light from the hall.

They were on her before she could make a move to defend herself...

15

Ted seized Gia's arm and hauled her out of the
room. Mark slammed the door and locked Peg
back inside.

"Come on. We've got trouble," Ted said,
releasing Gia's arm.

Relief washed over Gia. The Dethboy costume
was making Ted and Mark think she was Wally.
Obviously, they hadn't found him yet.

Gia followed Mark and Ted around a corner and
ran into someone coming their way. Gia recognized him immediately.

The *real* Dethboy stood before her.

Dethboy laughed. "Deitz, that outfit just
doesn't look as good on you as it does on me.
Take it off."

"I don't take orders from you," Gia said, the
voice box at her throat making her sound just
like the real Dethboy. "Besides, I have to go
back to Peg. She's losing it again, and I've
got to calm her down."

Ted nodded. "Remember that first night? She
yelled so much I didn't get any sleep."

Dethboy folded his arms. "Yeah, I wish we didn't have to do it this way."

Gia was surprised. Dethboy and the others didn't seem thrilled by what was going on. She was glad her mask hid her reaction.

Gia turned to Ted. "You said there was some kind of trouble?"

Dethboy was the one who answered her. "We took Darren tonight, like we were supposed to. But on the way over here, he got away from us."

"We need to pull out," Mark said. "Darren got a pretty good idea of where we were heading. He knows this place real well."

"It's not secure," said Ted nervously.

"We have to move Parrish and Straus," Dethboy said. "Deitz, let's go talk to Faceless and get the okay."

Gia thought fast. She couldn't go back to the computer room with them. The minute they saw Wally, her cover would be blown. "I'll take care of it. This place has to look completely dead, just in case anyone comes around. One of you stay here and guard Peg. The other two go outside and bring in whoever's watching the back door now."

"I don't think so," said Dethboy. "We need somebody outside."

Gia glared at Dethboy. "Don't question what I say. Just do it!"

Ted started to look panicked. "Don't act like that with us. *You* don't have anything to lose compared to us if—"

Dethboy spun to face Ted and fixed him with a stare. Ted immediately fell silent.

That's odd, Gia thought. Ted had started to say something that Dethboy didn't want Wally to hear. They were all in this thing together, and Wally even appeared to be Faceless's right-hand man. What would everyone in the Fraternity except Wally know?

Dethboy turned back to Gia. "No problem, Deitz," he said with a shrug. "You're the boss. Or should I say, the boss's *pet*."

The other guys laughed. Gia ignored them and headed back toward the computer room.

"Go get 'em, Danger Deitz," one of them muttered.

Gia just shook her head. The police would be here soon, and now there'd be no one outside to turn them away. The library would look deserted, just like she'd told them. All she had to do was keep everyone from leaving and hope that Faceless arrived in time for the party.

Behind her, Dethboy called, "Hey, Deitz. How'd you get all that mud on your shoes? You've been in here for two days straight."

Gia froze. The woods she'd crossed to get here had been damp and muddy.

Don't panic, she thought. Stay cool.

"Thanks for reminding me," Gia said, turning to face them. "*You* losers weren't watching the back door when I went out to stretch my legs. And you *still* weren't there when I came back in."

"So that's what it was," said Ted. "I thought I heard someone come in before. I—"

Ted suddenly fell silent. Gia saw confusion on their faces. She tensed as she heard a foot-step behind her.

"Take off the mask, Gia."

Gia's shoulders slumped as she turned to face Wally. He stood with another guy Gia had never seen before. Slowly, she pulled off her mask.

"All right, Gibson!" Dethboy said mockingly. "You almost got us with that one!"

Wally glanced at Dethboy. "Enough. What Gia said was right. We *do* need to make this place look deserted. Mark, take care of it."

"Okay," Mark said. He headed down the hall.

Wally looked at the other two. "Ted, D.B., find a room for Gia—and don't turn your back on her."

With that, Wally turned and headed back to the computer room with the guy who'd apparently freed him.

"Wally, why are you doing this?" Gia called after him.

Wally didn't answer. Dethboy nudged her arm. "Come on."

Gia, Ted, and Dethboy started down the hall. Gia looked over at Dethboy. "So why don't *you* take off your mask?" she asked.

"He never takes off his mask," said Ted. "We'd all like to know who's under there."

Gia thought this was strange, but didn't say anything.

They came to an empty room. Dethboy gestured for her to go in.

"And don't try anything stupid," Dethboy said. "I don't want to hurt you."

Gia laughed bitterly. "I got a different idea the other night, when you were chasing me across campus."

"You were meant to get that idea," Dethboy said. "But if I'd really wanted to catch you, I could have. That's why I tripped and fell. So you could get ahead. And I'm sorry about what happened in the bell tower. No one ever meant for you or anybody else to get hurt. That wasn't part of the plan."

"I bet Peg would like to hear that," Gia said, stepping into the room.

"You're probably right," said Dethboy. "That's why we're making sure you can't tell her anything."

Dethboy turned to Ted. "Stay here and keep her quiet."

Ted nodded, then closed and locked the door. He looked over at Gia. "Sorry about that complaint I had to file against you," he said. "I'm sure you're probably an okay person."

Gia nodded, not really listening. Suddenly, she remembered who was talking to her. Ted Leonetti. She knew something about his father that would surprise him. Something she'd printed out from the Fraternity disk Faceless had intended for her to take to the authorities.

Gia knew there was a chance she could overpower Ted, but if she failed, he would never listen to anything she had to say. She had to try reasoning with him first.

Gia smiled at Ted. "I'm sure your dad's probably an okay person, too. He just did what he had to, right? So that he could take care of his family. The embezzling, I mean."

Ted's face went white. "How'd you know about that?"

Gia took the printout from her pocket and slid it across the floor to Ted.

"This was on the disk Faceless wanted me to take to the police," said Gia. "There was a file on Mark, too. A whole bunch of files, as a matter of fact."

"No way," Ted said, his shock turning to anger as he read the printout. "Faceless said we were done after this!"

"Oh, yeah," Gia said. "You'd be done, all right. Totally. Faceless was setting you up. You and everybody in the Fraternity."

"Even Deitz?"

Gia shook her head. "There wasn't a file on him."

"But this doesn't make sense," Ted said. "Faceless wanted the cops looking for the Lurker, not us."

"Really?" asked Gia. "Who was supposed to move Peg and Adrian before the cops could get here?"

"Dethboy." Ted said it slowly, as if something terrible had just occurred to him. "He was supposed to go first, make sure everything was safe. Then he was going to call us…"

"I don't think so," Gia said. "Faceless has to convince the cops that there's an on-line menace here at Wintervale. Someone who finds things out about people, then uses that knowledge to control them. Isn't that what Faceless has been doing to you? The authorities would find you guys, but not Peg and Adrian. And what would you tell them?"

"That someone on-line made us do it."

"Right," said Gia. "By turning you guys over to the cops, Faceless would make sure they'd believe my story. The Lurker uses different names all the time. Faceless. The Lurker. The police would just figure it was one person behind it all, playing some kind of twisted game. That's what I thought it was at first, too."

"Oh, man…" Ted said. He looked at the piece of paper again. His hands were shaking. "You—you *could* have just found this somewhere."

Gia shook her head. "There was a camera in my room. Someone here was watching me. Were they taping me, too?"

"Uh-huh."

"That video would show me pulling this up from the disk I found at the pep rally. Who was monitoring the video?"

"Dethboy."

"Right. And I'll bet if you checked, that tape would be erased right now. Because none of you guys are supposed to know that Faceless is planning on betraying you."

Ted started pacing. "Dethboy said the tape was accidentally erased. We never saw it. Oh, man…" He shook his head. "Faceless said one job, and we'd all be free."

"All of you?" Gia asked.

"What do you mean?"

"What about Wally? Faceless doesn't have any-thing on him, right?"

"That's right," said Ted. "We're not supposed to let him know that we're being forced to help. As far as he's concerned, we're a bunch of heroes."

Gia nodded. "I think Wally knows who Faceless is. If you'll help me, I think I can get him to tell us. Then no one will have to worry about what Faceless has on them. Because we'll have something on Faceless."

"Taking Peg and Adrian," said Ted.

Gia nodded. She didn't want to tell Ted about the impossible situation she was facing. The police would be here any minute, and she was now certain that Faceless wasn't going to show. Faceless would gladly sacrifice all of the pawns in this game rather than be revealed. And if she was right about Wally, he didn't deserve the fate that was about to come crashing down on him. None of the Fraternity did. They had all been forced or tricked into this.

All except Dethboy.

Gia waited anxiously as Ted thought over what Gia had told him. Finally, he nodded.

"Come on," said Ted, unlocking the door and darting into the hallway. Gia raced after him. Together, they hurried to the computer room. Mark and Dethboy had gathered there with Wally and some guys Gia didn't know. Wally was pounding at his keyboard.

"I don't know what's wrong," Wally said. "I just can't make the connection."

Dethboy looked up and saw Gia and Ted. "Leonetti!" he said. "What do you think you're doing?"

"Faceless is using us," Ted said.

One of the guys laughed. "No kidding."

Gia stepped forward. "You don't understand.

Faceless is going to sell all of you out."

"It's true," Ted said, raising the printout. "She's got proof."

Wally hit a button on his keyboard, then rose to face Gia. "I'm sorry about all this, Gia. But—"

"They're all being forced into this by Faceless," Gia interrupted. "Faceless has something on every one of them and is using the information to control them. Just like the Lurker."

Wally looked around the room at the other members of the Fraternity. Many of the guys couldn't meet his eyes.

Dethboy started for Gia. "None of us need to hear this! You're going back into lock-up. And so's Leonetti!"

"Wait!" Wally yelled.

Dethboy hesitated.

Wally crossed his arms over his chest. "I want to hear what else Gia has to say."

Gia told her story quickly. By the time she was done, Wally had sat back down, a shattered look on his face.

"You know who Faceless is," Gia said quietly to Wally. "Don't you?"

Wally looked up at her with hollow eyes.

"Tell us," Gia said. "Do it now, before it's too late."

Suddenly, the silence in the room was broken as harsh sounds erupted from the computer. A voice spoke through the electronic synthesizer.

"Wally?"

"It's over, Faceless," Wally said. "We know everything."

The voice came again. "I don't think you do know everything, Mr. Deitz. This isn't Faceless. This is the Lurker..."

16

The voice of the Lurker echoed through the room, disguised by the synthesizer. "Five minutes ago, one of my operatives made a personal visit to Faceless. You were very helpful with that, Gia. Thank you."

"What are you talking about?" Gia demanded. She looked around the room at Wally, Dethboy, and the other members of the Fraternity. "I didn't do anything to help you."

"The mechanics of it aren't important," said the Lurker. "All that matters is that the call you made from the library to an acquaintance of mine gave me your location. Once I pinpointed the library, I had a fixed point to begin my computer traces. Oh, and Wally, the scramblers you're using are out of date. The software changes just about every day. One has to keep up with these things."

Gia glanced at Wally. He seemed drained. No one spoke.

"As of this moment," the Lurker continued, "everyone who was under Faceless's control is now under mine. I know everything that Faceless knew—and more."

Ted shook his head. "Faceless promised we'd be free if we did what we were told!"

"Faceless is no longer in a position to keep that promise," the Lurker said. "And at the moment, you have more important matters before you. Dethboy, are you there?"

"Yes," said Dethboy.

"Four police cars just entered the campus. I suggest you get Peggy Parrish out of there before the police arrive. If she's found in the library, you'll all be going to prison, where you'll be worthless to me. Take Peggy somewhere else. Anywhere else. Now."

"I understand," Dethboy said, heading down the hall.

"And if Ms. Gibson does anything to try to stop him, I'd suggest that the rest of you stop her."

"What about Straus?" asked Mark.

"He won't talk," the Lurker said. "I give you my word on that."

Gia felt a sudden chill. "Aren't you worried about what I'll say to the police when they get here?"

"Not at all," the Lurker replied. "No one will

believe you now that the Fraternity has destroyed your reputation. You've got no cred- ibility at Wintervale. Say what you like. Everyone else here will say they were having a little party. Right, everyone?"

Gia watched the guys nod their heads in defeat. "Yeah, right," they muttered. Only Wally remained silent.

"That's it?" Gia asked. "But I'm still expelled. Everyone thinks I'm crazy. I'll never get into another college..."

"Ah, Gia," said the Lurker. "It doesn't have to be that way. If you're willing to do a favor or two for me, I'm sure I could—"

Suddenly, the Lurker's voice shorted out. Gia spun around and saw Wally holding the computer plug he'd just disconnected from the wall. He approached Gia slowly.

"What'd you do that for?" Ted asked.

"So I could do this," said Wally. Spinning around, he grabbed Ted and shoved him toward the other members of the Fraternity. "Run, Gia!" Wally cried. "Stop Dethboy if you can!"

Gia bolted from the room. She heard yelling as Wally held off as many of the Fraternity as he could, followed by the footsteps of those who slipped by him. They were coming after her!

She turned a corner, trying to find the room where they were keeping Peg. Just ahead she saw Dethboy carrying Peg in his arms. Peg seemed out of it—Dethboy must have chloroformed her.

Dethboy headed for the back door. Gia ran after him. He was moving fast, even with Peg in his arms.

Dethboy kicked open the door and ran toward the woods. Gia heard sirens coming. If she didn't stop Dethboy now, it would be too late.

Gia burst through the rear door of the library. Dethboy was just a few feet ahead. She had to slow him down. Closing the distance between them, Gia hurled herself at Dethboy, leaping onto his back. She wrapped her arms around his neck, her legs around his chest.

Dethboy stumbled back and sank to his knees, unable to support the added weight. Peggy slipped out of his arms and tumbled to the ground. Gia heard her moan and breathed a sigh of relief. She was okay.

With a cry of rage, Dethboy reached back and tried to grab Gia. She tightened her hold around his neck and pulled back. Dethboy gasped for breath. Gia drove him forward, into the soft earth.

Beams of light shone on her. Gia looked up and

squinted into the bright headlights of police
vehicles. The Fraternity guys who'd been following her darted back into the library.

Dethboy tried to lift himself up, but Gia's
hold was weakening him. "Got ya," she whispered into his ear as he struggled for breath.
Behind her, Gia heard car doors slamming. From
the corner of her eye she saw police officers
coming their way.

"Nobody move!" someone shouted.

Ignoring the policeman, Gia yanked off Dethboy's mask.

The first thing she saw was a man's short
cropped red hair. In front of her was Brian
Donachy, head of Wintervale campus security.
Gia sat back, suddenly exhausted, as the
police officers closed around them.

Groggily, Peg rose to her knees. "You saved
me!" she cried, throwing her arms around Gia.
"I was so scared!"

Gia looked up at the police officers. She
could tell from the way they were looking at
her that it was going to be all right.

That night, for the first time in what seemed
like forever, Gia slept without nightmares.

*   *   *

The next day, Gia left her dorm room and was greeted by Jenny in the hall.

"Hey!" cried Jenny, walking over. "Good going," she whispered. "You beat him. I didn't think anyone could."

Gia smiled. This was the real Jenny, not the smug sorority queen. Old pom-pom head was human after all. "How's it going?" she asked.

Jenny let out a deep breath. "I'm dealing. There's a chance my sorority might let me back in. My parents are still trying to get back on their feet, money-wise. We'll be okay."

Gia looked around to make sure no one was listening. "I'm sorry the Lurker did all that to you. It was the Lurker, wasn't it?"

Jenny nodded.

"He shouldn't be able to get away with it," Gia said. "You were just trying to help me. You didn't do anything wrong."

"It's done," said Jenny. "There's not much either of us can do about it. We just have to keep going, right?"

Before Gia could respond, Marissa came down the hall and joined them. "I knew you'd come out of this okay!" she said to Gia.

"Thanks," said Gia. "Look, I've got to be somewhere. I'll see you guys later."

"Okay," said Marissa.

"See ya!" said Jenny.

After making her way across campus, Gia sat down near the fountain and waited. People kept coming up to her and calling her a hero. The news of Donachy's capture was all over campus.

"For those of you just tuning in," came Val's voice, as someone walked by with a radio, "our very own chief of security Brian Donachy was arrested last night. Apparently, he was keeping a student, Peg Parrish, locked up at the old library. The details are still unclear, but the important thing is that Gia Gibson came to the rescue. Pretty good for a fresh-man. Way to go, Gia!"

There'd been no mention of the other students involved, Gia realized. And there wouldn't be, either. The Lurker had made sure of that, just like he'd made sure that Donachy was blamed for everything that had happened.

Just then, Wally came up to Gia. He looked at her nervously. "Mind if I sit down?"

She shook her head and waited in silence. Wally had asked to meet her. He could do the talking. Finally, he cleared his throat and said, "I don't blame you for being angry—"

"Angry?" Gia burst out. "Everybody that I trusted, everyone that was supposed to be my friend, turned on me. And you're the worst. You were in on it from the beginning!"

Wally looked away. "I thought I was doing the right thing," he said. Then he turned back to her. "What exactly happened last night with you and the police? I was still inside the library. I got the basics, but—"

Gia shrugged. "Before I could tell the cops anything about Faceless and the Lurker, Donachy confessed. He said that he took Peggy and made those boys file complaints about me. That he did it all on his own."

Gia shook her head. "Whatever Faceless had on Donachy, it must have been pretty bad. Donachy knew that if I could convince the cops about Faceless and the Lurker, it would all come out. He was willing to ruin his career and go to jail rather than risk that."

Gia paused for a moment. "I didn't have any hard evidence. It was my word against everyone else's. Even Adrian backed Donachy up. So I went with what Donachy was saying. And now everybody thinks I'm some kind of hero."

"You are," Wally said.

Gia shrugged. "The dean came down to the police station last night to see me. He apologized. He heard that Donachy had forced those

three guys to file complaints against me. When
they were questioned, Ted and the other two
backed up Donachy's story."

Wally nodded.

"So I get to stay at Wintervale," Gia continued. "And Peg'll be out of the hospital this
afternoon."

"That's good," Wally said. "I'm glad."

"And now it's like it never happened," Gia
said, frustrated and angry. "The Lurker wins.
He gets everybody in the Fraternity as an
operative. Everybody except you."

Wally looked tense.

"I think I know why you didn't come forward
last night," Gia continued. "I mean, if you
had, the two of us could have told the police
the truth. We could have backed each other up.
Faceless didn't have anything on you. That
means the Lurker can't hurt you now. But you
were still protecting Faceless, weren't you?"

Wally was quiet a moment. "Gia, there was no
way we could have proved anything. Like you
said, there was no hard evidence. It would
have been our word against the word of more
than a dozen people. We wouldn't have stood a
chance. That's why you went along with what
Donachy was saying. And so did I."

Gia shook her head. She was angry, but she knew Wally was right. Then she thought of something. "Was Peter in on it?"

"He didn't have a clue," said Wally. "Gia, listen to me, okay? I wanted to see you today because there's something important we need to talk about. Like you said, the Lurker doesn't have anything on me. Or you, for that matter."

Gia looked at him, wondering where he was going with this. "Uh-huh..."

"We're free of the Lurker. But a lot of people aren't. They need our help..."

Wally spoke for almost five minutes. When he was done, Gia stared at him in disbelief. He wanted to take down the Lurker, and he wanted her help. His idea was clean and simple. It might even work. But the cost was so high...

Gia shook her head. "Not a chance. You must be crazy."

"I'm serious. This is important."

"Forget it," said Gia. She got to her feet. "I'm out of it now, and I'm staying out. I still don't even understand half of what's been happening."

"Gia, wait!" Wally said. "What do you want to know?"

"All right," said Gia. "Here's an easy one. One I know you have the answer to. Who's Faceless?"

Wally turned and scanned the quad, then pointed to a couple arguing in the distance. "Take a look."

Gia shaded her eyes. The woman had dark hair and wore a green-and-yellow Wintervale University sweater. The man was…

"Adrian?" Gia asked. "You don't mean…"

Wally shook his head. "Not him. The woman."

Gia watched as Adrian stormed away from his companion. She followed, looking as if she was pleading with him. Gia didn't recognize her.

"I don't get it," said Gia.

"Adrian told you about his girlfriend. The one Dethboy took a year ago. He was telling you the truth—or what he thought was the truth. That's Adrian's girlfriend. She is Faceless."

Gia's heart thundered as the couple drew closer. She was struck by the woman's dark eyes and wild black hair. She looked like a panther, sleek and beautiful, and ready to attack at any moment.

So you're Faceless, Gia thought. You're the

person I have to thank for everything I've been through.

Although she'd never seen the woman before, Gia knew her name all too well. She stood up and yelled, "Rebecca!"

The woman turned. When she saw Gia, her expression grew cold.

Wally touched Gia's arm. "Let it go. The Lurker's already done more to her than you ever could."

"I doubt that," Gia said. She broke from Wally and started toward Rebecca...

17

Gia strode toward Rebecca. She had no idea what she was going to say, but she had to do something. Suddenly, Adrian stepped in front of her. "Hold on," he said.

"Get out of my way," Gia said, looking past Adrian's shoulder at Rebecca's expressionless face.

"I'll meet you later," Adrian said to Rebecca.

As Rebecca walked away, Gia looked into her eyes and was startled by how hollow they were. Defeated.

Gia glanced back at Wally. She wondered why he wasn't running after Rebecca. Could it be that he didn't want anything more to do with her?

Gia looked at Adrian's handsome face. "You had me fooled all along," she said bitterly. "I guess your acting classes are paying off."

"Let me explain," Adrian protested. "Please." He gestured toward the bell tower in the distance. "We could go to one of our usual places."

Despite herself, Gia laughed. "Let's make it the theater instead."

"You got it."

She allowed Adrian to lead her to the theater.
Auditions were being held for a new play. Gia
and Adrian sat down near the back.

"When I spoke with Goldeneye on-line—" Gia
began.

"That was the Lurker. Every time."

"You're one of his…?"

"No. The Lurker promised me that he'd find out
what happened to Rebecca and make sure it
didn't happen to you. In return, I did some
things he asked me to, like contact you. And
I let him use my screen name. I let him be
Goldeneye."

"And you told him what we talked about," Gia
said grimly. "So that when I was on-line with
Goldeneye, I'd think it was you."

Adrian nodded. "I was desperate. I really
thought Rebecca was gone. She was my whole
life."

"What about now?" Gia asked.

He shook his head. "I don't know. When I went
on that climb with Ted and his buddies, I
never really expected to see Rebecca again. I
just wanted to know the truth. They chloroformed me while I was packing for the hike. I

woke up in the old library and Wally was there. He told me that Rebecca was alive. That she was behind all this. And it all started to make sense. If I wanted to keep her from going to jail, I'd have to play along."

"Were you really a prisoner?"

"Oh, yeah. Wally wanted me to know that Rebecca was okay, but he couldn't take any chances. I was just so grateful that she was alive, I would have agreed to anything."

"That's why the Lurker was so sure you wouldn't talk to the police," said Gia.

Adrian nodded. "When the police hit the old library, Wally came and let me out of the room. I just blended in with the other guys. The police talked to us one at a time. Every one of us told the cops the same story—we were there on a fraternity prank. We never saw Peg and Dethboy—he must have been taking her out of the building."

"So when was the big reunion? You and Rebecca?" Gia asked.

"Last night. Around midnight. She came to my dorm room. She told me everything she'd done and why."

Gia nodded. "So answer my question. How do you feel about her now?"

"I'm not sure," he said slowly. "She used me. She let me think she was gone. To her, it was all for a higher cause."

"Bringing down the Lurker."

"Right. But…I don't know. How can you do that to someone you care about? I'm not sure I ever knew her at all."

Gia suddenly found herself thinking about Wally's idea to get the Lurker. "Tell me about Rebecca," Gia said. "Why'd she do it?"

"She was going to be an actress. She was great at putting on masks. And using people. It wasn't hard for the Lurker to pick her out. He told her they'd be partners. And for a while, that was true. You wouldn't believe the things they did together to people on this campus. If the truth came out, it would have been enough to send Rebecca to jail—which is what the Lurker told her one night. She didn't think they were partners after that. Even though he told her she was his right-hand man, it didn't matter. She was just being used, like all his other operatives."

"Too much…" Gia said, seeing how easy it was for the Lurker to target anyone he wanted.

"Rebecca wanted to break free. She knew about Wally and quickly figured out how to control him. He wanted to be a hero, so she told him how. The day she disappeared, Rebecca and Wally made a run at the Lurker. Rebecca kept the Lurker on-line while Wally used a program to invade the Lurker's system."

"What were they looking for?" asked Gia.

"All the secrets he was using to manipulate his operatives. And information that would reveal who the Lurker really was. But it wasn't there."

"And the Lurker found out what they were doing," Gia finished for him. "I bet he wasn't too happy."

"Rebecca was sure that he was going to turn her in to the police. She faked her own disappearance—she'd been setting it up all along, just in case. She gave up her identity and went into hiding. After a while, she figured out a way to come back and take down the Lurker. Her plan would have worked, too—if she hadn't let her need for vengeance get the better of her."

"What do you mean?" asked Gia.

"Think about it. All she had to do was go to another college and put together her Fraternity, then return to Wintervale and collect some students. Send a message to the police and the press, pretending to be the Lurker, taunting them to catch him. But she wanted the Lurker to see it coming. He did. And he got her."

Gia suddenly had the feeling that she was being watched. She spotted someone looking her way. Lee. The moment their eyes met, he turned and vanished through one of the exits.

"I've got to go," Gia said, getting up to follow him.

Adrian grabbed Gia's hand. "I really am sorry."

"I know," Gia said as she hurried away. She went outside and caught sight of Lee. He was headed toward Crane Hall. When she got back to the dorm, Lee was waiting for her outside her door.

"Are you here to apologize? Or to deliver a message?" Gia asked.

"Both," said Lee.

They went into her room. He booted up her computer, then logged on to the campus net. From there, he went into a private room. It seemed to be empty.

"Just log on," Lee said. "He's there."

"Wait," Gia said. "Were you ever really my friend? Or did the Lurker put you up to it from the beginning?"

"I'd like to think I'm still your friend," Lee said.

Gia glared at him.

Lee looked down. "I didn't know anything was going on until we were at the party. Darren filled me in. He said—"

"I don't want to hear it," she said. "We'll talk some other time."

"Okay," said Lee. "Some other time." He left her alone in her room.

Gia looked at her screen. No, not quite alone. She started typing.

> **Ripley:** What do you want?
> **Goldeneye:** I wanted to make sure there were no hard feelings. What happened to you was nothing personal.

Nothing personal…Gia had heard that phrase one too many times.

> **Ripley:** You know what's funny? For a while there, I almost felt sorry for you. I even started to think you were the good guy, and that Faceless was the bad guy. When I woke up this morning, I wanted to know who Faceless was and I wanted to make Faceless pay. But none of this would have happened if it wasn't for you. I almost wish Rebecca had pulled it off.
> **Goldeneye:** Don't challenge me, Gia. You have no idea what you're getting into. Do you know what I've done with Rebecca? She

has her old job back. The one thing she
wanted most in the world was to get away
from me. Now she's right back where she
started. Only it's worse than before.
Because now she knows that there's no way
out. And she's no longer my right-hand
man. That position's still open. Interested?
Ripley: I don't think so.

Gia realized that Wally was right. The Lurker's punishment for Rebecca was far worse than
anything Gia could ever imagine. Strangely
enough, the knowledge didn't make Gia happy.
Instead, she was starting to see that Rebecca
may have had the right idea all along—though
she went about it in the wrong way. There was
no doubt about it. The Lurker was a monster.
And he had to be stopped.

Ripley: I understand now that you're the
problem. And you're not as hard to get at
as you think you are.
Goldeneye: I'm the problem? Whatever.
Just don't fool yourself into thinking
that you're the solution.
Ripley: Don't worry. You're not worth the
effort.

Gia turned off her machine before the Lurker
could respond. She had the feeling that he was
one of those people who always wanted to have
the last word. And she wasn't going to give it
to him.

An hour later, Gia was on her way to class when a tall man with a beard came up to her. "Gia Gibson, right?" he asked.

She nodded.

"Dan Washburn, reporter." He held a card out to Gia.

She looked at it. The name of the biggest newspaper in the country was printed on the card. "What can I do for you?" she asked excitedly.

"I heard about what happened to you here. We want you to write a story for us. An account of what you went through."

"Really?" Gia asked. She could hardly believe it. Washburn was offering her the one thing she wanted most in the world: to be a journalist for a major newspaper. Best of all, there were no strings attached. Or were there?

"Just give me a call when you're ready," said Washburn. Gia couldn't help noticing that he seemed a little nervous. *She* was the one who should be nervous.

"Sounds great," Gia said.

The reporter looked relieved. "Gia, this'll put you on the map," he said. "Every paper in the country'll want you. And I'll help. Whatever you need, you got it."

Something the Lurker said about Rebecca came back to Gia. *She's no longer my right-hand man. That position's still open. Interested?*

No way, Gia thought, telling herself that she was just being paranoid.

"After all," said Washburn, "I mean, it's the least I can do for my alma mater, right?"

Maybe. Or maybe not. Gia forced a smile. "That sounds great. I'll put some notes together."

"Excellent. You won't regret this."

"Thanks," said Gia. "Speak to you soon."

She hurried off to class. But after class, she'd find Wally...

* * *

In a dark room, the Lurker sat before a computer monitor. The entire day had gone by, and so far, Gia Gibson hadn't called the reporter. She would make an excellent addition—but first, she had to take the bait.

Suddenly, an e-mail came in. It wasn't from the reporter. It was from Gia. The Lurker was startled. Gia didn't know how to make direct contact...

But Wally Deitz might be able to figure it out. The Lurker opened Gia's e-mail.

To: Goldeneye
From: Ripley

Guess what? You were almost off the hook. I was going to walk away, but you couldn't leave me alone. Washburn blew it. I know you sent him. I know you like playing games, but this was a bad move. Now it's my turn.

See ya...soon.

The Lurker stared at the screen, wondering what to make of Gia's message. She couldn't possibly be serious. A challenge?

Then again, if she had Wally on her side...

Turning to the keyboard, the Lurker typed a message to Darren and Lee. Gia Gibson and Wally Deitz had to be found. Now!

But even as the Lurker sent the messages, a grim feeling settled in.

The Lurker sensed that it was already too late...

*   *   *

It was night, and the bus was heading to a place far from Wintervale University. Wally and Gia sat in the back. They were the only passengers. The driver was listening to the radio.

Sometime in the next few hours, Gia and Wally would get off the bus before it reached its destination. They would make their way to the nearest airport and pick a destination at random. Paying for the trip would be no problem. Wally's trust fund had seen to that.

"Are you sure about this?" Wally asked.

Gia looked out the window and nodded. She watched the road disappear behind them.

"We'll have to change our names and the way we look," said Wally. "Give up our lives. Become faceless, just like Rebecca."

"I know."

"And contacting our families is going to be tough. Not impossible, just difficult. The Lurker will be on the lookout for that kind of thing."

"Wally, do we have to talk about this right now?" Gia asked. "I'm exhausted."

They rode along in silence for a while.

"Gia?" said Wally.

"Um-hmm?"

"Do you think you can ever forgive me for what happened?"

Gia took Wally's hand and held it tight. "I wouldn't be here if I hadn't already," she said.

He squeezed her hand and smiled.

"There's just one thing," Gia continued. "I don't want to use the Lurker's own tactics against him. I remember this Nietzsche quote from philosophy. Something about, when you fight monsters, make sure you don't become a monster yourself. That's what happened to Rebecca. It *can't* happen to us."

Wally nodded. "I'll watch your back."

Gia smiled. "I'll watch yours." Suddenly, she started to laugh.

"What?" Wally asked. "What's so funny?"

Gia settled back in her seat. "I'm just picturing the look on the Lurker's face when we come back and knock on his door. Her door. Whatever. I can't wait."

"Yeah," said Wally excitedly. "Neither can I…"

They rode into the night, their journey only just beginning…

Lost Episode

One year earlier…

Val entered the party wearing a black leather micro-mini, a tight white halter top, and stiletto heels. She grinned as she saw a bunch of guys checking her out—and a bunch of their girlfriends giving her dirty looks.

She'd barely gotten in the door when she spotted a drop-dead-gorgeous guy on his way over to her. He was lean and muscular, his bare chest covered in tattoos. He had long, blond, wavy hair, a square jaw, and sparkling blue eyes. Val liked what she saw.

"I've seen you around," he said.

"That's possible. I've been around." She laughed. "Don't take that the wrong way."

"Wouldn't dream of it. 'Course, I've never seen you up here in Malibu before. You usually run with the L.A. crowd, right?"

"First time for everything. I guess I was just in the mood for something different tonight."

He smiled. "Want me to show you around?"

"You won't hear me complaining."

They walked through the beach house. At first glance, the party looked like every other college bash. Loud. Cramped. Crazy. Though Val was only in high school, she'd been to a ton of college parties and knew the territory pretty well.

"So what's the deal?" asked Val, trying to sound cool. "A friend of mine said this was an Extreme party, whatever that means."

He handed her a drink. "It's simple," he explained. "Check out those two in the corner." He nodded toward a guy sitting on the floor, a pretty blonde on his lap. They were making out as if tonight were their last night on earth.

"What about them?"

"That's Gavin. The girl he's with is Susan. She isn't his girlfriend."

"Okay. So where's his girlfriend?"

He nodded at another couple near the double doors leading to the pool. They, too, were having a fine time exploring each other's dental work. And more.

Over the guy's shoulder, Val saw a young African-American woman with auburn dreadlocks and a skin-tight pink dress homing in on her tour guide. Great. Just what she needed. Competition.

Suddenly, a scruffy-looking guy wearing an eyepatch and a black leather trenchcoat scooped the woman up in his arms and carried her out to the pool. Val watched as he dumped the giggling young woman into the water, then leaped in after her.

As the tour went on, Val saw some things that were kind of shocking, but even more intense were the offers and invitations she received. But she didn't let any of it faze her. She'd needed to get out tonight more than ever. Anything to get away from what was waiting for her at home.

"So what's your name?" Val asked.

"What do you want it to be?"

She smiled. This one liked playing games. Good. "I changed my mind. No names."

"Saw something on my way in. Wanna check it out with me?"

"Sure."

He took her hand and led her to a private room in the back of the house. The moment they were alone in the darkened room, Val expected her companion to start kissing her. In fact, she'd been looking forward to it from the moment she first saw him. Instead, he turned on the lights and sat down before a computer.

"I came here to break some boundaries," said Val. "Not play kids' games."

"Come on, Val. Who's talking about kids' games?"

Val froze. She hadn't told this guy her name.

He seemed to read her mind. "I told you, I've seen you before. At other parties. Rob Foster's. Jackie DuPrey's. I asked about you. All I could find out was your name."

She relaxed. "I like to be mysterious."

"Works for me." He booted up the computer.

Val smiled and fingered the mousepad absent-mindedly. The last thing she wanted was for this guy to figure out she was still in high school.

"Come here," he said. "I've got something I think you're gonna like."

She went to him, watching over his shoulder as he entered some kind of chat room. The green on black lettering leaped out at her.

"What's that?" she asked.

"The Ratskellar. A private chat room on the Wintervale University net. Ready to break some boundaries?"

"Show me."

Val chose the screen name Isolt and started typing. When her on-line companion chose the name Tristram in her honor, she was flattered.

The party no longer existed for her. Even her nameless boyfriend and the unfulfilled promise of a tryst with him slipped her mind. She was vaguely aware of him standing behind her as she typed away, touching her hair, her shoulders. Kissing her neck. One moment his arms were around her. The next he was gone.

There was only Tristram and Isolt. What they did together that night was unthinkable.

*   *   *

The next morning, Val got up early to check the morning newspaper. She still had a few minutes before she had to get the twins out of bed and start breakfast. Ever since her mom had gone away and her dad had fallen to pieces, she'd been stuck with taking care of the house and everyone in it. Thank God for Sam. If it wasn't for her older brother, she'd be trapped in the house forever. Whenever she did get away, she always made up for lost time.

Val wondered what Sam would think if he knew that his perfectly responsible little sister was the same bad girl who was getting a rep on the party circuit.

He'd never believe it. Just like he wouldn't believe that she had anything to do with the story on page three.

FAMOUS HOLLYWOOD PRODUCER CHARGED WITH BLACKMAIL, EXTORTION.

Her heart raced as she skimmed the article. Everything she'd done last night with Tristram had been real. He'd shown her proof that this producer was a crook and dared her to tell the guy on-line that she was going to expose him.

And then she did it. She went to the Feds. Tristram promised he would keep her safe. He swore it.

"I'll protect you."

And he had.

*   *   *

Isolt: So what's it gonna be tonight?
Tristram: That's up to you. There's another party on Friday. Go there. Pick someone. Find out what you can about them, but be subtle.
Isolt: Then what?
Tristram: Come back to me. We'll figure out something.

Val loved Encino. The party was a blast. She was kind of hoping to see her nameless tattooed friend from Malibu, so they could pick up where they left off. But he wasn't around.

His loss.

Val found someone else easily enough. Tall, dark, good-looking in a George Clooney sort of way. He was with someone else at the time, a dark-haired biker chick, but he was barely noticing her. His eyes were on Val most of the evening.

The moment his date was in the ladies' room, the George clone came over.

"And here I thought I'd seen it all," he said.

"You hadn't seen me," Val said.

"Just what I was thinking. You got a name? A phone number?"

"Uh-huh."

He waited. She liked making him wait. A wide smile lit up his handsome face. "You gonna tell me?"

Suddenly, the biker girl was back. She grabbed her boyfriend's hand and yanked him away. "Just check in the Yellow Pages under 'Escorts.' Or try a 900 number. You know you want to."

"Later," the boyfriend said as he was dragged off.

Val was stunned. That little witch! Val wasn't really trying to steal her boyfriend. She was just having some fun. Well, this wasn't the end of it. Not by a long shot.

A little while later, Val made her way over to the couple and said, "Hey, handsome. Hey, whatever you are. I haven't seen you around."

"My name's Mike," the guy said, holding out his hand. Val took it. She was hoping he'd kiss her hand. Praying for it.

She wasn't disappointed. The biker chick's face turned red.

"Don't you have a street corner or something where you normally do this sort of thing?" the biker chick asked.

Val took a long time looking her up and down. "Well, if I did, I bet I'd get a lot more business than you would, honey."

"Like that's saying much."

"Why don't you ask him what that's saying?" she said, nodding toward her boyfriend.

He couldn't take his eyes off Val.

She leaned in close to the biker chick. "In case you didn't get that, it means he's bored with you. And just to set the record straight, *he* came after *me*. It's not my fault you can't keep him interested—"

Someone brushed against the biker chick from behind. Drink in hand, she lurched forward as if she'd been shoved. Coke splattered all over the front of Val's halter top.

"Oops, I'm sorry," said the biker chick. "That was an accident. You know about accidents, right? Like you being born. An accident."

Steaming, Val went off to the ladies' room. A friend met her inside. Sophy. A sophomore at UCLA. Tall and leggy, kinky brunette hair. Deep brown eyes. Wearing a black dress with a jacket.

"Did you see what just happened?" Val asked her friend as she squeezed the Coke out of her halter top.

"Uh-huh."

"What can you tell me about that dear, sweet little creature?"

Sophy laughed. "Other than the fact that you want to wring her neck?"

"Yeah."

"Her name's Calle Ann Copeland. She has relatives in the area—she's visiting. Lives in

New Orleans. The guy's her boyfriend."

"Not for long," said Val.

"What are you gonna do?"

"About him? Nothing. He's probably making like a vulture and circling around some other girl by now. But her? Plenty." She looked down at her top. It was ruined. "What am I gonna do?"

Sophy stripped off her black jacket. Val put it on. It was a tight fit, but maybe that wasn't such a bad thing. "You're gonna have a good time, like you always do. And don't worry about Calle Ann. You know what they say. What goes around comes around. Eventually."

Val nodded, but somehow, eventually couldn't come soon enough.

> **Tristram:** She's a hot-shot programmer in New Orleans. A high school senior, like you.
> **Isolt:** How'd you find out so much?
> **Tristram:** It's easy if you know how. Maybe someday I'll show you.
> **Isolt:** I want you to.
> **Tristram:** In the meantime, are you up for another dare?
> **Isolt:** Try me.

Val tacked the article up on her wall at home, right next to the one about the producer. In the new clipping, a once prominent actor had

been caught cheating on his wife. Some slimy
detective had taken a photo. The picture
showed the actor ducking out of a cheap motel
with an unidentified woman.

The woman's face in the photo belonged to
Calle Ann Copeland. The photo was a fake, of
course. Created digitally. Flawless.

Two hundred copies of the article had been
sent to Calle Ann's hometown. The local mayor
got one, along with a page from the high
school yearbook with Calle Ann's entry cir-
cled. Her parents got one, along with everyone
on her block.

It was classic.

And now, as far as Val was concerned, they
were even for the fiasco at the party. She
just hoped for Calle Ann's sake that she would
be a little more careful the next time she
decided to take someone on...

*　　*　　*

Months flew by and Val couldn't get enough of
Tristram's dares. It was becoming a game, she
realized. Only she didn't know the rules, or
what she might get if she won.

She didn't care, either.

One night, when Tristram was busy, Val spent
the entire evening staring at her Wintervale

University application. She'd filled it out weeks ago and stuck it in a drawer. Every now and then she took it out and stared at it. She didn't know why she tortured herself with it. So long as she was stuck playing mommy to the twins, she'd never be able to leave home.

College? Sure, as long as it was a local one.

She was trapped.

*　　*　　*

"Honey, we need to talk."

All Val could think about was going to bed. She couldn't even remember how many nightclubs she'd been to tonight. What was her father doing up, anyway?

"Sorry it's so late——" Val began. She started to take off her raincoat, then remembered the skimpy dress she was wearing. The coat was wet but she knew she'd better keep it on till she got upstairs.

Her dad smiled—something she hadn't seen him do in so very long…

"She's coming home, honey," said Val's father. "Your mom's coming home!"

That night, Val took out her Wintervale University application, slipped it in an envelope, and put a stamp on it.

She was going to get her life back. It was about time.

* * *

Val's first week at Wintervale was incredible. The school was perfect. Everything that Los Angeles was not.

She'd half-expected Tristram to show his face. If he was really a guy.

It never happened.

> **Tristram:** You don't miss the excitement of L.A.?
> **Isolt:** Maybe a little. UCLA's one of the best film schools around, and I want to be a producer some day, but you and me, we're gonna make some noise here, right?
> **Tristram:** You bet. Starting with KLRK.
> **Isolt:** What's that?
> **Tristram:** The new college radio station. And it's all yours. Or it will be, once your show is on the air.
> **Isolt:** Me? A DJ? I love it! One of these days, Tristram, you're gonna have to come out from behind that screen. I can think of a lot of ways to thank you.
> **Tristram:** We'll see, Isolt. We'll see...

* * *

"As I live and breathe!"

Val turned and was stunned to see Calle Ann Copeland standing before her. If the phony picture wasn't still in her scrapbook, she would have forgotten what the girl looked like by now.

"Surprised to see me?" Calle Ann asked. "You should be. I know what you did. It's one of the reasons I'm here."

"I don't know what you're talking about," Val said. On the outside, she was calm. But inside...

"Don't worry. I wouldn't choose a college just for payback. If things work out, that'll be a little added benefit." Calle Ann winked. "See ya!"

They didn't speak again for months.

*   *   *

As the first semester came to an end, Val couldn't believe how her popularity had swelled. She was happy and free. There were risks, of course. Everything she did with Tristram was dangerous. But that was part of the thrill.

She'd never felt so alive. A shame Tristram had been so distant lately. Something was bothering him. Though he'd never admit it, Val had the idea that the entire Faceless incident had left him shaken. She wished that there was something she could do.

It wasn't that she loved Tristram...but she felt
a loyalty to him. No matter what games they
played, he'd always been fair with her.

She went into the Rat. It wasn't long before
they met up in a private room.

> **Tristram:** I have news.
> **Isolt:** Don't you always. Shoot.
> **Tristram:** I forced your mother to come
> home.

Val felt the room suddenly grow cold.

> **Isolt:** What are you saying?
> **Tristram:** I found out things about her.
> Told her that if she didn't go home and
> play the perfect wife and mother, she
> would regret it.

Val felt as if she'd been struck. Tristram's
words were brutal, yet they made sense. Val
believed what he was telling her.

> **Tristram:** You're only here because I want
> you here. Cross me and I'll let your mom
> off the hook. Then you'll have to go
> back. You'll be trapped again, just like
> you were.

The chill Val felt quickly turned to anger.
But she held it in.

Isolt: Why are you telling me this now? I didn't betray you.
Tristram: No, you didn't. And now you know that you can't.

Val turned her computer off.

So that was it, then? Tristram was just using me.

"That can work both ways," she said as she rebooted her computer and went back on-line. Choosing a new screen name was simple enough. She knew just the one.

Val typed it in:

Vader

Yes, she was trapped. Just like all of the Lurker's operatives. She didn't like it, and one day, she would find a way to pay the Lurker back for questioning her loyalty.

In the meantime...

She smiled as she headed into the Rat, wondering if anyone would be foolish enough to accept a dare.

The game's just begun—see how it turns out in *Know Fear*...the story of Josh Stewart, who's transferring to Wintervale for second semester. Check it out!

KNOW FEAR

Intro

The music could be heard halfway across campus. It was Saturday night—party night—at the frat. Colonel Mustard was jamming to a packed house, and Val was doing a live remote. She got up onstage as the band finished their first set.

"Hey, all you maniacs out there!" Val shouted into her mike. "This is the night we've all been waiting for. 'Apocalypse Man' Josh Stewart is ready to defend his title against Lee 'The Crusher' Farris. Come on up, boys!"

Josh and Lee pushed their way through the crowd and leaped up on stage. Lee snatched the wireless microphone from Val's hand.

"You're goin' down!" Lee bellowed, getting in Josh's face. "You're goin' through the floor, you're goin' through the basement, you're journeying to the center of the earth, pal!"

Josh laughed. "Hey, he's not as dumb as he looks," he said to the crowd. "He can actually tell up from down!"

Everyone roared. Lee snarled and did his best Incredible Hulk imitation.

Val grabbed the mike. "It's been nine straight victories for 'Apocalypse Man' Josh Stewart since 'Dangerous Darren' McKiernan took him on a month ago. He's set records, he's broken them!"

The crowd cheered. Josh raised his hands and grinned.

Life was good.

Val leaped down off the stage. "Any last words before we bring out the instruments of destruction?"

Josh took the mike and said, "I'd just like to thank my tutors. My grades are looking good! As of this Friday, I'm off the bench and in the game!"

Val took back the mike. "All right! You've seen his moves in 'Apocalypse Man,' now you'll see them on the basketball court. Way to go, Josh!"

The crowd broke into loud applause. "Enough talk!" Lee screamed. "Let's get it on!"

Colonel Mustard started playing. A couple of guys wheeled out two PCs on carts from the computer room. Josh and Lee sat down at their stations, facing each other as if they were about to play Battleship.

Suddenly, a young blond woman came up to Josh, holding a copy of the student newspaper. It was open to Josh's weekly column, "Notes from Apocalypse Man." She held out a pen. "Would you sign this for me? I'm Amy."

"You bet," he said, signing the column.

"This is like...so cool!" she said, giving him a quick kiss on the cheek.

"Will you stop embarrassing yourself?" said a brown-haired woman wearing a biker jacket.

Amy went to join her friend. "Relax, Calle Ann. That's Josh Stewart."

"I'm *so* impressed," Calle Ann said.

Suddenly, a deep voice rumbled out of the computers.

"IT IS NEW YEAR'S EVE, 1999. A GROUP OF FANATICS KNOWN AS THE CABAL HAVE ATTACKED THE PRESIDENT AND STOLEN THE FOOTBALL—THE BRIEFCASE KEPT NEAR THE PRESIDENT AT ALL TIMES. IN THE BRIEFCASE IS A DEVICE THAT CAN LAUNCH EVERY NUCLEAR MISSILE IN THE UNITED STATES.

"THE CABAL LEADERS HAVE TAKEN OVER THE UNITED NATIONS BUILDING AND ARE CLOSE TO BREAKING THE CODES TO START THE APOCALYPSE. YOU MUST SHATTER THEIR DEFENSES AND REACH THE

TOP FLOOR, WHERE THE FOOTBALL HAS BEEN TAKEN.

"YOU HAVE ONE HOUR.

"GOOD LUCK."

"Try not to break your joystick, big guy,"
Josh said. He wished he felt as confident as
he sounded.

"Worry about yourself, Stewart. This won't be
what you're used to."

The game began. On the screen before him, Josh
saw a long, narrow hallway that branched off
to the left and right. He moved forward, then
spun and yanked his joystick all the way back.
His point of view shifted to show him the
ceiling. Two bizarre creatures looked down at
him. They wore black and looked like something
out of *The Fly*.

Spider-Ninjas. He hated these guys. The game
didn't normally get this tough this fast. Usually, he would run into human enemies first:
Men in Black wearing mirror shades and carrying heavy-duty pulse cannons. Josh was outfitted with a set of futuristic armor that would
keep him safe for several hits but would ulti-
mately give out. After that, he'd have to pick
up Enhancers.

But first things first. There was only one way
to take the Spider-Ninjas out of the game.
Each had a hidden hot-link that tied them into

the Cabal's master computer and kept them
anchored in our world. There was no explanation in the game for where these monsters came
from. Other dimensions. Other worlds. But if
you could hit the target, they were pulled
back.

The Spider-Ninjas leaped down from the ceiling. Josh fired at them with his Disabler as
he drove himself back into the wall. He knew
from his many visits to this level of the game
that there was a soft spot in the wall behind
him—an area where reality had been warped by
the appearance of his monstrous enemies.

Josh sank into the wall and went out of phase.
The Spider-Ninjas attacked, but their hairy
arms went right through him. Josh pulled to
the right, hoping to put some distance between
himself and his attackers before becoming
solid again.

But there was nowhere to go—the layout of the
game had been changed! The soft spot in the
wall was now much smaller than it had been. He
could only move forward, right into the arms
of the Spider-Ninjas!

Suddenly, a figure wearing metallic blue armor
appeared behind the Spider Ninjas and opened
fire. It was Lee.

The Spider-Ninjas exploded in bright neon
flashes as Lee hit their targets. "You're
making it too easy, Apocalypse Man!" Lee

called from his computer. "That's the last time I save your butt!"

Josh's opponent backed down the corridor and vanished. People in the crowd started booing.

"I thought Stewart was supposed to be good!" someone called out. Others started chanting Lee's name.

Josh didn't like the idea of losing, but he had to admit, Lee was good.

Damned good. Bolting out of his safe zone, Josh became flesh and blood again. He raced blindly after Lee but ran into more Spider-Ninjas. Men in Black. Crimson Marauders. Flying Fiends. Hungry Elevators.

Josh was torn up pretty bad by the time he found a pack of Enhancers and saved himself from a pair of Steel Wolves. He reached the third level in ten minutes, playing his worst game ever. It was a miracle that he'd survived this long. Dumb luck.

"Hey, Apocalypse Man!" shouted Lee. "Watch what's around the next corner!"

Josh tried a desperate tactic. Running up the wall and onto the ceiling, he turned the corner and fired the last rounds from his Disablers.

But nothing was there.

"Some champion!" Lee called out, disgusted.

Josh froze as Lee's blue-armored warrior charged forward, his Disabler blazing. Flashes of bright blue light arced in Josh's direction. There was nowhere to run.

"Squash him like a bug, dude!" someone yelled. "Do it, Lee!"

Desperate, Josh pulled back on his joystick—but his character leaped forward!

Josh was startled. What was that? A system error? He didn't have time to worry about it. He jammed on his joystick. His character raced forward, then stopped an instant before Josh pulled back on his joystick. It was eerie. As if someone else was playing the game for him.

A hailstorm of Lee's Disabler fire passed right through him—Josh was in a soft spot in the ceiling.

Lee cursed and moved forward, showering Josh with more suppression fire. Josh ejected his own empty weapon as Lee appeared directly below him.

At just the right moment, Josh jammed the joystick down and dropped onto Lee, grappling with him. He quickly stole the other player's weapon and opened fire. Lee dove out of the way, grabbed Josh's empty Disabler, and ran.

Josh rushed after him, hoping to end the game quickly now that things were going his way again, but Lee was gone.

The game lasted five more minutes. Lee managed to find Disabler charges to defend himself. For a while, it seemed that Josh and Lee were evenly matched. But whenever Josh was in trouble, his "guardian angel" helped him out.

Every time it happened, Josh was tempted to just release his joystick and quit the game. Either the system had gone berserk or he had gone berserk—or someone else was involved in this. It felt like cheating to Josh, and he wanted no part of it.

Still…He'd played most of the game without help. And if he lost the title, things could go back to the way they'd been. Fast. Josh Stewart, "Nowhere Man." He'd been all that back home in Salem—and not much of anything here at Wintervale. Until he'd started playing this game, no one knew he existed. Could he give that up so easily?

After two more skirmishes, Josh took Lee out of the game. Moments later, he was taken out himself by a large group of Cyber-Gnomes and Men in Black.

"Ladies and gentlemen, boys and girls!" Val cried, holding up Josh's hand. "Apocalypse Man!"

The crowd exploded. Josh smiled. But in his heart, he had a sick feeling. He didn't like what he'd done tonight. Not one bit.

"You got lucky," Lee said before heading off with a couple of his pals.

Darren came over to Josh as Colonel Mustard started rocking. "You put on a great show," Darren said. "For a while there, I thought it was over for you."

"So did I," said Josh.

Darren laughed.

Josh looked around and noticed Jenny for the first time. He'd met her on summer vacation and fallen for her. Fallen hard. If it hadn't been for Jenny, he'd never have come to Wintervale in the first place. Now she was with some other guy, as if what they'd shared hadn't meant anything to her.

She walked past him and patted his cheek. "Hi…Bye."

Jenny disappeared into the crowd, her date following close behind her. Josh wondered why she was acting like this. Even if they weren't going out, they could at least be friends.

Couldn't they?

Josh said good-bye to Darren and headed back to his dorm room. When he got there, he booted up his computer. An e-mail had just arrived.

To: Apocalypse Man
From: Ozymandias
Didn't mean to leave you stranded during the first part of the game. We need to talk. Meet me in Room E off the Rat.

Josh had suspected that someone had been helping him tonight. Now he had proof. He logged onto the Ratskellar—good thing Darren had gotten him in. Quickly, he found Room E. Someone was waiting.

Ozymandias: Tough game, huh, Josh? I know it's not easy keeping up a winning streak.

That sounded like a threat. Josh had a bad feeling about this. Sure, he liked being Apocalypse Man. But there was no way he'd let someone hold it over his head.…

Apocalypse Man: You're the one who deserves the title. I'll step down if you want.
Ozymandias: That's not what I want. You may not realize it, but you're getting better with every game. I'll help you as long as you need it. No strings attached.

Josh didn't buy it.

Apocalypse Man: Who are you, anyway?
Ozymandias: Just someone who tries to do some good around here. There're a lot of bad things going on at Wintervale. Things most people don't know anything about. I do what I can to keep this place safe, but sometimes I need help. Think you might be up for it?

Josh really didn't like the sound of this. Still, he wanted to know more, so he decided to play along. For now.

Apocalypse Man: When do we get started?

SCOTT CIENCIN

Okay, so it's like this: I'm sitting at my computer, minding my own business. Trying to make a deadline. All of a sudden, an e-mail comes in. I read it, even though I don't recognize the screen name. It says, "You've had 22 books published. Some under your name, some under Richard Awlinson and Nick Baron. In fact, it was your using pen names that made me think you might be the one!"

I was a little skeptical. Especially when this character promised me fame and fortune. (I'm still waiting.) But he said that he was a fan. He'd read the Forgotten Realms™ novels SHADOWDALE and TANTRAS I'd written as Richard Awlinson. He'd also liked The Elven Ways, Book One: THE WAYS OF MAGIC, as well as the Dinotopia books WINDCHASER, LOST CITY, and THUNDER FALLS. And he's psyched to read GODZILLA: KING OF THE MONSTERS and my upcoming hardcover thriller, LIGHTNING UNDER GLASS.

So he started telling me about what he was doing with these students at Wintervale University, and I was hooked. Just like Darren and Jenny, I've got a weakness. I want to be a BIG FAMOUS WRITER. The Lurker knew it. That's how he got me to write about his adventures. So who is the Lurker? You think I know? If I did, I'd be tracking him down, too. ;-)

LURKER
TRACKER™

Access denied?

Feeling left out because the
WINDOWS are closed to you?

Send in this coupon for your *free* MacIntosh version of the
LURKER TRACKER disk today!

❏ **LURKER TRACKER DISK**
   (0-679-88602-8)

Order it now, and you can read Wintervale student profiles—
and their secret diaries! Photos included! You wouldn't want
to miss the Lurker's letter, his Commandments and the
opportunity to store clues in the Lurker Tracker and guess
the Lurker's identity!

Name _____

Address_____

City _____**State**_____**Zip** _____

Please send $3.00 for postage and handling to:
Lurker Tracker, 400 Hahn Road, Westminster, MD 21157.

Please allow 4 to 6 weeks for delivery.

Need your free Lurker Tracker even faster?
Call toll free 1-800-793-2665 to order by phone—
you can charge the postage and handling.
Please mention interest code (049-02) to expedite your order.

"Yahoo accepts us for who we are. We like that."

Do You Yahoo! ?

Check out Yahoo! at www.yahoo.com

Yahooligans!™

The Web Guide for Kids at www.yahooligans.com